# *Praise for* Shadow Baby

"McGhee avoids all treacle, letting things unfold with a sure-handed narrative discipline that makes her story all the more charming. She leads readers to the novel's sad-but-satisfying conclusion, never losing the emotional balance that makes this tale a signal achievement." —*Minnesota Star-Tribune*

"A feisty little heroine who often seems equal parts Huck Finn, Eloise, and . . . well, maybe Shakespeare's Beatrice-to-be. . . . At once witty, tender, funny, touching, and, by the end, tragic in a way that perfectly brings all to a close, if never to an end. Bound for success, or else the world has gone mad." —*Kirkus Reviews* (starred review)

"Loss, guilt, and regret are conquered and transformed. . . . With a mix of deadpan humor and pathos, McGhee perfectly captures the voice of a sensitive, wise child on the cusp of adulthood, at once knowing and naïve." —*Publishers Weekly*

"Tender . . . full of unforgettable, rich characters, McGhee's second novel will move many readers by its beauty and simplicity and by its implicit hopefulness." —*Library Journal*

"McGhee's work, full of contrasts and transformations, is a strong, solid novel with quiet feminist undertones. Virginia Woolf would be proud." —*Booklist*

"At last, a heroine to root for! In this charming novel, Alison McGhee has opened a new window on childhood."
—Hilma Wolitzer, author of *Summer Reading*

"Bright, funny, and almost spookily imaginative, Clara, by her own admission, is a student of the laws of nature, an expert in the ways of hermits and pioneers, an 'apprentice' to life. That she is also eleven years old is probably the least important fact about her; she's an old soul. . . . Alison McGhee, with her seductive, almost hypnotic prose, has created a heroine that one simply must love."
—Judith Guest, author of *Ordi*

"McGhee writs about childhood
grace. Poignant and bittersweet, l
—William Gay, author of *The*

# ALSO BY ALISON McGHEE

*Falling Boy*

*Snap*

*All Rivers Flow to the Sea*

*Was It Beautiful?*

*Rainlight*

# Shadow Baby

by Alison McGhee

THREE RIVERS PRESS
NEW YORK

Published in the United States by Three Rivers Press, an imprint of the
Crown Publishing Group, a division of Random House, Inc., New York.
www.crownpublishing.com

THREE RIVERS PRESS and the Tugboat design are registered trademarks
of Random House, Inc.

Originally published in hardcover in the United States by Shaye Areheart
Books, an imprint of the Crown Publishing Group, a division of Random
House, Inc., New York, in 2000, and in paperback in the United States by
Picador, a division of MacMillan Publishers Ltd., New York, in 2001.

The Reading Group Guide by the author included here first appeared
on the Picador website in conjunction with the first paperback edition
of this work.

Library of Congress Cataloging-in-Publication Data

McGhee, Alison, 1960–
Shadow baby / Alison McGhee.—1st ed.
I. Title
PS3563.C36378 S53 2000
813'.54—dc21        99–047315

ISBN 978-0-307-46228-2

Printed in the United States of America

10 9 8 7 6 5 4 3 2 1

First Three Rivers Press Edition

*This book is dedicated to
Don and Gaby and Laurel and Holly and Doug,
and to the sweet memories of
Christine McGhee and Marty Walsh.*

# Acknowledgments

For lending her keen writer's eye to this book in its formative phase, not to mention every other draft I sent her way, I thank fiction writer and friend Julie Schumacher.

My gratitude to Tom and Kitty Latané, of T&C Latané Metalworking in Pepin, Wisconsin, for their generosity in sharing with me a bit of their artistry in the ancient craft of metalworking.

Thanks also to Bill O'Brien for his support in the writing of this book, and to Ellen Harris Swiggett for the constancy of her friendship.

Profound thanks to Shaye Areheart, editor extraordinaire, and Doug Stewart, friend and agent, believers both in the art of possibility.

# PART ONE

In all metalworking operations, the workpiece is permanently deformed, sometimes very severely. A major object of metalworking theories is to permit prediction of the amount of deformation, and the forces required to produce this.

From *An Introduction to the Principles of Metalworking*

# Chapter One

Now that the old man is gone, I think about him much of the time. I remember the first night I ever saw him. It was March, a year and a half ago. I was watching skiers pole through Nine Mile Woods on the Adirondack Ski Trail, black shapes moving through the trees like shadows or bats flying low. I watched from the churchhouse as my mother, Tamar, and the rest of the choir practiced in the Twin Churches sanctuary.

That was my habit back then. I was an observer and a watcher.

When the choir director lifted her arm for the first bar of the first hymn, I left and walked through the passageway that leads from the sanctuary to the churchhouse. The light that comes through stained-glass windows when the moon rises is a dark light. It makes the colors of stained glass bleed into each other in the shadows. A long time ago one of the Miller boys shot his BB gun through a corner of the stained-glass window in the back, near the kitchen. No one ever fixed it. The custodian cut a tiny piece of clear glass and puttied it into the broken place. I may be the only person in the town of Sterns, New York, who still remembers that there is one stained-glass window in a corner of the Twin Churches churchhouse that is missing a tiny piece of its original whole.

It's gone. It will never return.

That first night, the first time I ever saw the old man, I dragged a folding chair over to that window and stood on it so I could look through the tiny clear piece of patch-glass onto the sloping banks of the Nine Mile Woods. Down below you can see Nine Mile Creek, black and glittery. You would never want to fall into it even though it's only a few feet deep.

I watched the old man in the woods that night. He held fire in his bare hands. That's what it looked like at first, before I realized it was an extralong fireplace match. Tamar and I do not have a fireplace but still, I know what an extralong fireplace match looks like. I watched the old man for what seemed like two hours, as long as the choir took to practice. The moonlight turned him into a shadow amongst the trees, until a small flame lit up a few feet from the ground. The small flame rose in the air and swung from side to side, swinging slower and slower until it stopped. Then I saw that it was a lantern, hung in a tree. An old-time kind of lantern, with candlelight flickering through pierced-tin patterns. I knew about that kind of lantern. It was a pioneer lantern.

You might wonder how I knew about lanterns. You might wonder how a mere girl of eleven would have in-depth knowledge of pierced-tin pioneer lanterns.

Let me tell you that a girl of eleven is capable of far more than is dreamt of in most universes.

To the casual passerby a girl like me is just a girl. But a girl of eleven is more than the sum of her age. Although it is not often stated, she is already living in her twelfth year; she has entered into the future.

The first night I saw him the old man was lighting up the woods for the skiers. First one lantern hung swinging in the tree, then another flame hung a few trees farther down. I stood on my folding chair and peeked through the clear patch-glass on the stained-glass window. Three lanterns lit, and four. Six, seven, eight. Nine, and the old man was done. I watched his shadow move back to the toboggan he had used to drag the lanterns into Nine Mile Woods. He picked up the toboggan rope, he put something under his arm, and he walked through the woods to Nine Mile Trailer Park, pulling the toboggan behind him. The dark shapes of skiers flitted past. The old man kept walking.

I watched from my folding chair inside the churchhouse. In the light from the lanterns I could see each skier saluting the old man as he walked out of the woods. A pole high in the air, then they were gliding on past.

He never waved back.

I pressed my nose against the clear patch of glass and then the folding chair collapsed under me and I crashed to the floor. My elbow hurt so much that despite myself I cried. I dragged over another chair and climbed up again. But by then the old man was gone.

The old man lived in Sterns and I live in North Sterns. A lot of us in North Sterns live in the woods. You could call a girl like me a woods girl. That could be a name for someone like me, who lives in the woods but who could not be considered a pioneer. Pioneer children lived in days gone by.

I started at Sterns Elementary, I am now in Sterns Middle, and in three years I will be at Sterns High. So has, and does, and will everyone else in my class. CJ Wilson, for example. CJ Wilson's bullet-shaped head, his scabbed fingers, the words that come leaking from his mouth, I have known all my life. Were it not for CJ Wilson, and the boys who surround him, I might have been a different kind of person in school. I might have been quicker to talk, faster to raise my hand. I might have been picked first for field hockey. I might have walked down the middle of the hallway instead of close to the lockers. I might have been known as a chattery girl. I might have had a nickname.

Who's to say? Who's to know?

Jackie Phillips wet her pants in kindergarten. We were in gym class. Jumping jacks. I looked to my right, where Jackie Phillips was jumping kitty-corner from me, and saw a puddle below her on the polished gym floor. A dark stain on her blue shorts.

Six years later, what do the students of Sterns Middle School think of when they think about Jackie Phillips? Do they think, Captain of Mathletics, Vice-President of 4-H, science lab partner of Bernie missing-his-right-thumb Hauser, Jackie Phillips whose hair turns green in summer from the chlorine at Camroden Pool, Jackie Phillips who's allergic to strawberries?

They might. But they will also think: Jackie Phillips wet her pants in kindergarten while everyone was doing jumping jacks. That's the way it is.

Does everyone look at me and think, Clara Winter who loathes and despises snow and cold, who lives with her mother The Fearsome Tamar in North Sterns, whose eyes can look green or gray or blue, depending, who has never met her father or her grandfather, who has represented Sterns Elementary at every state spelling bee since first grade, whose hair could be called auburn, who loves books about days gone by? Clara Winter who saw that Jackie had wet her pants in gym class and so stopped jumping jacks and ran out of line and tried but failed to wipe up the spill surreptitiously with a used tissue before anyone else would notice? Is that what they think?

They do, and they do not.

The eyes, they know. That I live with my mother Tamar in North Sterns, they know. The spelling, they know. The fact that I, as a kindergartner, got Jackie Phillips's puddle all over my fingers from trying to wipe it up, they know. These are the things they know.

You see how much is left out.

Some may not even know about Tamar. Tamar is what I call my mother, but only when she's not around. I tried it once in front of her.

"Good morning, Tamar," I said. "Any Cheerios left?"

She gave me a look.

"Clara Winter, what the hell are you up to now? Is this another of your weird word things?"

I tried to look ingenuous, which is a word I believe to be a perfect word. Only certain words fit my personal category of perfection. What makes the word *ingenuous* perfect is the way the "g" slides into the "enuous."

"What? What do you mean, Tamar?"

She couldn't stop laughing. That was the last time I did that. To her face I call her Ma mostly, because that's what pioneer girls called their mothers. That's what Laura Ingalls

Wilder called her mother. I'm the only girl I know who calls her mother Ma.

You might wonder why a girl of eleven would be interested in an old man. You might think that a girl of eleven would have time only for her fellow sixth-graders. You might assume that the life of an old man who lived alone in a trailer in the Nine Mile Trailer Park in Sterns would hold no interest for an eleven-year-old child.

You would be wrong.

After the first night, when the old man lit lanterns in Nine Mile Woods, I saw him everywhere in Sterns. I saw him in Jewell's Grocery buying noodles and a quart of milk when I was there buying a lime popsicle. I stood behind him in the checkout line and observed his movements. The old man gave Mr. Jewell forty-five cents—five pennies, one quarter, one dime, and one nickel—and Mr. Jewell gave him a Persian doughnut. The old man reached into his pocket and took out another penny, which he dropped into Mr. Jewell's "Take a Penny, Leave a Penny" cup.

"Thank you, Mr. Kominsky," Mr. Jewell said. "And what can I do for you, Miss Clara?"

I waited until the old man had walked out of Jewell's and down the sidewalk toward Nine Mile Trailer Park.

"I would like to know Mr. Kominsky's first name," I said.

"Mr. Kominsky's name is George," Mr. Jewell said.

"Thank you."

I left Jewell's and walked across the street to Crystal's Diner, where Tamar was waiting for me.

"There is an old man who lives in the Nine Mile Trailer Park who will soon become my friend," I told her. "That is my prediction."

Tamar sucked her straw full of milkshake, then suspended the straw above her mouth and let it drip in. That's a habit of hers.

"Well, far be it from me to argue with a Clara Winter prediction," Tamar said.

That's Tamar. That's a Tamar remark. Tamar's mother died when she was eighteen years old. On Tamar's seventeenth birthday, her mother gave her a black and red and orange lumberjacket that Tamar still wears despite the fact that the seams are ripping, the zipper keeps breaking, and moths have eaten holes in the wool.

When I first spoke to the old man, I told him that my last name was winter, which I always keep in small letters in my mind, so it doesn't gain in importance. Winter is something that should be lowercase, in my opinion. Winter is to be feared. Winter is to be endured. That's what I believe to be true.

"Hello," I said. "I'm Clara winter. I was wondering if I could do my oral history project with you."

No answer. He stood there behind his screen door, looking at me.

"It's for my sixth-grade project."

No answer.

"I'm eleven."

Why did I say that? Why did I tell him I was eleven?

"I saw you lighting lanterns. You like lanterns."

Babbling! But when I mentioned the lanterns, he let me in. Interview an elderly person, they said, find out all about their lives. It's called an oral history. The minute they assigned the oral history project I knew that I would interview the old man. I wanted to listen while he told me about lanterns. I wanted him to be my friend. I wanted my prediction to come true.

"I'll do Georg Kominsky," I said. "He lives in the Nine Mile Trailer Park."

I had already found his name in the telephone book. *Georg*, not George. He wasn't on the approved list. They had a list of Sterns residents who had been oral historied in the past.

"He's an immigrant," I said. "He's old."

Was he? I didn't know, but they love old immigrants. The old man was also a plus because Tamar, my mother, goes to choir practice every Wednesday night at the Twin Churches, exactly opposite Nine Mile Trailer Park.

"I've never been in a trailer before," I said when the old man let me in.

I took the liberty of walking around. It was a very narrow place. I had the feeling that if the old man, who was tall, laid down on his back crosswise, he might not fit without having to crumple up a little. Each end of the trailer was curved.

"Sir, is this what being on a boat's like?" I asked the old man.

Already I was getting used to him not talking. I liked the sound of my voice in his trailer. There was something echoey about it.

"I've always wondered what life on a boat was like," I said. "The smallness of it."

I walked straight to the end of the trailer, past the tiny kitchen with the miniature refrigerator and the miniature sink, past the little room with the sliding curtain-door that had a bed built onto a wall platform and drawers built into the opposite wall, into the tiny bathroom at the end that had a miniature shower, an ivory toilet, and a dark-green sink.

"I like your dark-green sink. It's unique. It's a one-of-a-kind sink, just like your house is a one-of-a-kind house."

"It's not a house," the old man said. "It's a trailer."

"Why do you think they're called trailers?"

That's when I first learned the trick of how to get the old man to talk. Just keep talking and once in a while throw a question in. He wouldn't answer and he wouldn't answer, and then he would answer.

"Do you want something to drink?" I said. "I can make you something to drink. I brought a selection of various beverages for you. Tea, instant coffee with instant creamer, and hot chocolate."

I had little bags of everything.

"I could make you some hot chocolate," I said. "It would be my pleasure. Miniature marshmallows already mixed in."

It was the end of March in the Adirondacks that night. We sat at his kitchen table and he stirred his coffee. Around and around he stirred. This is the kind of thing I think about, now that the old man is gone. I submerged all the miniature marshmallows in my hot chocolate until they disappeared. They dissolved. They were no more. You could say I killed them.

"Let me ask you a question," I said. "Say you're on death row. How would you rather die: electric chair or lethal injection?"

That used to be one of my favorite questions. I used to ask it of everyone I met. The old man stirred his coffee.

"If you had to choose, that is," I said.

"Did they tell you to ask that question for the oral history?"

"Yes."

He kept on stirring.

"Actually, no," I said.

There was something about the old man. Even though it was my habit then to tell untruths, around the old man I couldn't.

"This would be for my own personal information," I said.

"Well then," he said. "Let me think about it."

I had hoped for an immediate answer. But immediate answers were not forthcoming from the old man. That was one of his traits.

The Adirondack Ski Club created the ski trail from Utica to Old Forge, fifty miles of cross-country skiing. The night I first observed the old man, they had just finished the portion that wound its way through Nine Mile Woods and up through Sterns. Would you find me skiing on that trail? Would you find me out on a winter night, a scarf wrapped around my face, poling my way through the snow?

You would not.

I had a feeling that the old man knew the power of winter. How did I know that? Because when I told him why I spell my last name with a lowercase w, he nodded. He did not question. I used to love that about the old man.

The first night I ever met the old man, sitting at his kitchen table, I read a book report aloud. You might think that seems like a strange thing to do. You might think, Tamar is right, Clara Winter is indeed an odd child. But still, there we sat, me reading, him listening.

They like us to read a book and do a book report on it once every two weeks. "Now that you're in sixth grade," they say. "Time to develop your critical faculties." Etcetera. I scoff at this. Their definition of a book and my definition of a book do not coincide. "Fifty-page minimum," they say.

What kind of book is only fifty pages long? A comic book?

It hurts me to see a book report. It's painful to me. Book reports are to books what (a) brown sugar and water boiled together until thick is to true maple syrup from Adirondack sugar maples, (b) lukewarm reconstituted nonfat powdered milk is to whipped cream, and (c) a drawing of a roller coaster is to a roller-coaster ride. Give me a *real* assignment, I say.

I like to read books one after another. *Immerse*—another perfect word—myself in a book and then *immerse* myself in the next book, and just keep going until there aren't any more books left to swim in. That's why I hate it when authors die. I cannot stand it. There will be no more books forthcoming from that person. Their future books died with them. In the past I have found a series of books and loved it so much that all I wanted to do was read and read and read those books for the rest of my life. Then I would find out that the author was dead. Had in fact been dead for many a year. This has happened to me several times.

You can see how much it would hurt me to write a book report every two weeks. I could do such a thing only to a book I hated. And why would I read a book I hated? Self-torture?

My only option is to make them up.

Besides, there're not too many unread-by-Clara-winter books left in the school library. It's a strange feeling, to walk down a row of books with your head bent so you can read the titles, and recognize most of them. *Amelia Earhart: American Aviator. Alexander Graham Bell: Inventor of the Telephone. George Washington Carver: American Botanist.* I like biographies. I like the early childhoods of famous people. Sometimes they're what you'd expect them to be, sometimes they're not.

I like reading between the lines of famous early childhoods.

My favorites are pioneers. Winter explorers. The kinds of pioneers who bore the burden of snow and ice, who faced the cold head-on. Winter is to be feared. But who thinks about that now? Everyone thinks we've conquered winter. Houses with heat, cars with heat, stores and schools with heat. They forget what it used to be like. They can't begin to imagine what it was like for the pioneers, with one small fire in an unchinked cabin, or how cold it must have been in the Indians' winter camps.

Imagine it.

We are close to death every winter day. What if the furnace went out and the electricity went out and the phone line went out and the blizzard raged so hard that the road was a pure whiteness, and you slowly burned up everything wood in the house, and then twisted newspaper into tight rolls and burned them like fast-burning logs, and then started in on your summer clothes and the sheets and towels and mattress stuffing and anything else that could possibly burn, and finally, even, tore all your books apart and burnt the pages, all the time jumping up and down to stay warm, dancing even, with all your winter clothes on? It wouldn't matter. You would die. No one thinks about things like that. They all feel so safe.

Not me.

"Would you like to read my fake book report?" I said. "I have it here in my backpack. It was completed just this afternoon."

The old man stirred his coffee with the handle of his spoon. He did not use the *bowl* of the spoon, as I have seen it referred to in books but never, not once, in real life.

"It concerns winter," I said.

"You read it to me," he said.

*The Winter Without End*, by Lathrop E. Douglas. New York: Crabtree Publishers, Inc., 1958. You need to make up a title that sounds possible and an author that doesn't sound impossible. I always put down a year from long ago, just in case they check. They'd never check, but still. You could always say, "Oh, you couldn't find it? That's because it's out of print." They'd be impressed that you knew what out of print meant.

"Ready?" I said.

"Ready."

*It was the longest winter that Sarah Martin had ever known. Growing up on the Great Plains, she had known many a stark December, many an endless January, and the bitter winds of February were not unfamiliar to her. She was a child of winter. But that winter—the winter of 1879—Sarah knew true cold.*

*The potatoes had long since run out, as had the cabbages and carrots buried in sand in the root cellar. The meager fire was kept alive with twists of hay. When the first blizzard came, followed every few days by another, Sarah's parents had been trapped in town. It was up to Sarah Martin to keep her baby brother alive and warm until the spring thaw, when her parents could return to the homestead.*

*The true test of Sarah Martin's character comes when her baby brother wanders into the cold in the dead of night. Sarah blames herself for this; she was too busy twisting hay sticks in a corner of the cabin to notice that he had slipped from his pallet next to the fire and squeezed his way outside. "He's only two years old," thinks Sarah. "How long can a tiny child survive outside in this bitter cold?"*

*Will Sarah Martin be able to find her little brother in time? Will she be able to rescue him from a fate so horrible that she cannot bear to think about it?*

*Did Sarah Martin have the foresight to dig a snow tunnel from the house to the pole barn where Bessie and Snowball are stabled? Or is there nothing beyond the cabin door for her beloved brother but blowing snow, bitter wind, and a winter without end?*

*Will Sarah have to face the responsibility of her brother's death?*

*Will her baby brother be forgotten by everyone but her?*

*Will she miss him her whole life long?*

*Read the book and find out.*

I live in North Sterns, in the Adirondack Mountains. Winter loves these mountains. Snow is attracted to them. Snow craves falling here. Snow falls on the young and the old, the quick and the dead, the CJ Wilsons and the Clara winters.

"Well?" I said to the old man after I read him my fake book report. "What do you think?"

He stirred his coffee so that it slopped into the saucer.

"What happened?" he said. "How does the story turn out?"

"Read the book and find out," I said.

Most of the time I give my book reports a happy ending. The teachers expect that. An unhappy ending would raise alarm bells in their minds. That's because most books for children have happy endings. Few end in tragedy. Few contain irredeemable loss.

You might wonder why a girl of eleven would want to be around an old man seven times her age. You might wonder why she craved his presence, what she was hoping to find in Georg Kominsky. You might wonder if she found it.

"Tell me how the story ends," the old man said when I finished reading the fake book report. "I would like to know what happens."

So would I.

# Chapter Two

S oon after I met him, I told the old man about my missing lantern earring. I was making toast for myself and mixing up the coffee in his mug. You had to put a saucer underneath it. That's how he drank his coffee. He poured the milk in and then he stirred and stirred and stirred with the handle of his spoon until it slopped into the saucer, and then and only then would he take his first sip. I soon learned that about the old man.

"My lantern earring has met a tragic end," I said.

Tragic is a good word. It would be a good name too, with that soft middle "g," except it's not a name. You couldn't name a baby Tragic. That would be a travesty, which is also a beautiful-sounding word. Travis is the closest you could come to that one.

"My earring shall not see the light of day again," I said. "Swallowed by the snow like Jonah was swallowed by the whale."

It was my favorite pair of earrings, tiny silver lanterns like the kind pioneers used to light their way in the barn at chore-time. They were a gift for my tenth birthday, before I ever met the old man. Once in a while Tamar used to give me earrings, but only tool earrings, in keeping with her theory that work makes you strong. I used to have a set of hammer earrings, a set of pickaxes, a pair of scissors, all made of silver. But I lost one of each set. That's what happens when you wear clip-on earrings. They disappear. I would never have lost my lantern if Tamar had let me pierce my ears. The one fell off, to be lost forever in the snow.

"Two more years before Tamar will let me pierce my ears," I told the old man. "A veritable lifetime." *Veritable* belongs to me. It's one of my words. I like the way all the syllables after the "ver" go mumbling into each other.

"Two years is not a lifetime," the old man said.

"Nay sir, but it is 730 days. If it's not a leap year."

That's one of my talents. I can add extremely quickly in my head. Let me tell you a secret. As long as people believe you're an extremely fast adder, it doesn't matter if you make a mistake. No one notices. I've gotten by quite a few times like that.

Even as I told the old man about it, gravity may have been pulling my silver earring down to the earth, the little lantern dropping crystal by crystal deeper and deeper into the six feet of snow piled beside the entrance to the old man's trailer park, which is where I lost it. Maybe it would rest on the frozen crust of the ground until the end of April. When spring finally came and all the snow melted, maybe then it would be carried away by flooding, swept into Nine Mile Creek, and from there into the Utica Wetlands, to sink into the swampy mud without a trace.

"Ne'er to be seen again," I said to the old man.

It all comes back to snow and cold.

• • •

The old man planned to make me a replacement for my lost lantern earring. He had the ability to do that because he used to be a metalworker. There were many things about the old man that no one ever knew. They were all inside him. People thought he was a silent man, but they were wrong.

"Please tell me about your occupation."

That was a question I asked him in the beginning, when I was still doing his oral history. It was straight from the oral history list they gave us. Did they not trust us to come up with our own questions?

"Metalworker."

I wrote all his responses down on my roll of green adding-machine paper from Jewell's Grocery: 3/$1. Mr. Jewell keeps them in a bin up near the register, things that are a little cracked, a little broken, maybe not wanted. Things that they think people aren't going to want, that's what goes in the bin. Like adding-machine paper: who's going to want green?

Sometimes I think of it as my bin.

"I lost my lantern earring," I told him. "I knew something was wrong. There was just a feeling, like something was missing that should be there. The unbalancing. That lantern earring was heavy."

I showed him the one earring that was left.

"Early American," he said.

"Maybe."

"No maybe," he said. "That's a traditional American copper or tin lantern pattern."

"It's sterling silver," I said. "It was my tenth birthday present from Tamar."

He examined it. He tossed it from hand to hand for a little while.

"Paul Revere," I said, when I saw that he had stopped talking again.

Paul Revere was an early American man. I figured it might get him back on the talking track. I used to do that sometimes, let a name or a word drop into the air in front of the old man's quiet face.

"I read his biography," I said. "I took it out of the school library."

There's a Paul Revereware factory right in Rome, just fifteen miles from Sterns. The factory has a galloping red neon horse on the front of it. At night it's very bright.

"It took Paul Revere a long time to get his first silver pitcher made small the way he wanted," I said. "He couldn't get the proportions right. He had to figure out how to reduce and enlarge proportions without destroying the inherently graceful line of the original silver pitcher."

I like to talk like that, which is the way certain books are written.

"Do most eleven-year-olds talk like you?" the old man said.

"Nay sir, I think not."

Pioneers may have talked like that. It's hard to know. They didn't have tape recordings back then. It's all speculation, how they really talked. That's why I started writing down the story of the old man's life, because he didn't talk to anyone else and there was no one else to listen anyway. There needed to be a record of his life. That is what I believed to be true.

"Do not forget, however, that I am not merely eleven," I said. "I am even now in my twelfth year."

He smiled. No one else would have noticed but me, because I'm the only one who knew the looks on the old man's face well enough to tell what was a smile and what was a grimace.

"I used to make lanterns," he said. "Like your earring but big. Tin, mostly."

"Tin?" I said. "Tin."

Not a good sound, tin. Too short. Too abrupt. Too *tinny*.

"How about aluminum?" I said.

"What do you mean, how about aluminum?"

"Like soda cans. Like tinfoil."

"There is possibility in aluminum too," he said.

*Possibility*. A five-syllable word. If every finger is a syllable, possibility uses one entire hand neatly and nicely. It takes a tinsmith, someone who knows sheet metal, to see the possibility in aluminum. After the old man said that I started seeing possibilities myself. I looked up aluminum and tin in the library. You can find out a great deal from one half hour well spent at a library. I tested the old man after I had done my research.

"What sort of metal is tin, and is it commonly used by itself?" I said.

"Soft, white, and no."

"What metal, when combined with tin, forms bronze?" I said.

"Copper."

"Tell me the melting point of tin."

"450. About."

He knew his stuff. The old man really knew his stuff when it came to sheet metal. That's why he had the capability of making me a matching lantern for my one remaining silver earring.

"I learned how to make real lanterns that look like your ear-ring when I was a child," the old man said. "Decorative tin lanterns."

There are people who would not have understood the old man when he said "decorative." There are people who would have gotten twisted up in the old man's pronunciation, gotten lost in the vowels and consonants, given up in despair.

Not me. I understood the old man. We were *compadres*.

The old man's father may have been a metalworker too, with a forge in a shed near their thatched hut. That's how I picture the old man when he was a boy, living with his mother and his father in a thatched hut with an open cookstove in it. Walls made of turf bricks. Every few years the old man's father repaired the thatched roof, or even tore all the thatch off and started again. Their hut was on a street with many other neighboring huts. Horses and wagons clopped up and down the rutted muddy road. No cars. All day Georg's father worked in his forge, pumping air at the fire to keep it hot, banging and pounding on metal things such as horseshoes and anvils.

Georg's father was the town blacksmith. After school, which lasted only half a day, Georg would come immediately home, eat the bread and butter that his mother had ready for him, and go directly to the forge. It was from his father that Georg learned all he knew about metalworking. Georg's father was a stern but kind teacher. He wanted his son to grow to love working with metal as much as he, the father, loved it.

"For a skilled metalworker there is always a job," he told his son Georg. "Learn the trade well and you will never go hungry."

Georg's father sometimes did favors for his friends, straightening a horseshoe or bent nails without charging. He was known in the village as a generous and honest man. A beggar could always find a hot meal at the home of Georg's mother and father. From his father Georg learned the tools of the metalworking trade and much more. When school was out for the summer they worked together from sunup to sundown, then they would put away their tools for the night and go next door, where Georg's mother had dinner and tea waiting for them. Glasses of hot tea, strong and plain for Georg's father, half-milk for Georg.

In this way Georg learned, without haste, the ways of metalworking.

His particular gift for decorative metalworking was discovered early, when he would take the scraps of sheet metal left over from one of his father's projects and turn them into beautiful and useful objects, such as miniature lanterns, cookie cutters, and candleholders. Anything that could be made from sheet metal, Georg could make and make decoratively. Friends and villagers soon noticed the unusually beautiful lanterns and candleholders coming from Georg's father's forge. When it was discovered that it was not his father, but Georg himself, who was the artisan, word quickly spread.

"He has the touch," they said.

The old villagers nodded knowingly. They had seen this kind of talent before, but rarely. Rarely, a child is born with the knowledge of past lives still in his fingertips. They believed that Georg was such a child, that he had lived a life before as a forger, as a craftsman, as an artist. In this life, the skills from the previous blended in his fingertips, allowing him to produce useful objects of great beauty.

Georg was known for his precision, his vision, and the way that everything he created was made to be used. He was destined to be a metalworker. It was the fate he was born into.

Is that a true story? It may well be. Who am I to say?

I started collecting aluminum cans for the old man. I still have them. There may be a use for them yet. There is possibility in them. When you have your eye out for them, they're everywhere. Aluminum cans can be found crushed on the sidewalk, placed upright against buildings, and in every large garbage can you walk past and most small trash cans as well. Almost every car contains the possibility of an empty aluminum can, rolling back and forth underneath one of the seats. You can find an aluminum can, drained of soda, stuck behind a stack of Wonder bread in the Bread/Cereal aisle at Jewell's. Not paid for, no doubt.

We started out as interviewer and interviewee, but that changed. There were things the old man and I knew about each other. After a while, I just visited him, *compadre* to *compadre*. I used to write down his life because much of the time he was in a dark lantern world. You could see it in his face. Somewhere, there might still be a person who wants to know about the old man's life. Somewhere, someone who doesn't know he's gone might still be looking for the old man.

"When we left we had a lantern with us," the old man told me that night.

"When you left where?"

"Our country."

"What country?"

"It doesn't exist anymore. This was a long time ago. This was before the war. It was snowing."

I wrote that down: *snowing.* I could tell it had been snowing hard by the look on the old man's face. His eyes were squinted the way eyes get when snow is driving into them. There are those who see beauty in snow. They like its whiteness, the way it shuts out sound. My mother Tamar is one of them.

"It covers the good and the evil," she says. "Everything is equal in the snow."

Every September Tamar lifts her face to the sky and breathes in to the bottom of her lungs. "Smell it, Clara," she says. "A September blue sky, and the smell of autumn leaves. There is nothing better in this world."

*Nay sir, I think not.*

Now that the old man is gone, I wish I had asked him about my chickens. That's one of my regrets.

My chickens used to live in the broken-down barn across the field by the pine trees. They lived there, scrabbling in the dark, maybe flying up to the posts they roosted on. They were there every morning, waiting for the feed and water to be flung at them through the bars. They may have plotted to kill me.

It's possible. It's entirely possible.

"Do you believe that chickens are inherently vicious?"

That's a question that I want to ask someone. Who can you talk to about insane chickens? Not Tamar.

Those chickens, they started out so cute. I got them last June, when it was warm, a few months after I met the old man. They came in a wooden box, Rhode Island Reds, two roosters and twenty-three hens. Peeping yellow fuzzy balls. They crowded against each other and sipped up chick feed with their sweet baby beaks. Tamar penned off a corner of the broken-down barn for them. I put in my old dollhouse to amuse them.

"Now don't go making pets out of those things," Tamar warned me. "You know you're going to end up killing and eating some of them."

"Don't worry, Ma," said I. "I'm not even going to name them."

I read somewhere that if you didn't name your animals you wouldn't care about them. That was not a worry anyway. Those chickens grew up mean. The cocks jumped on my back every morning and every night. They dug into my skin through my shirt and pecked my head. Horny yellow beaks pierced my scalp and made my hair streaky with little lines of blood. Tamar did not go out to the broken-down barn. She spent a morning out there fixing up the pen, then she said: "This is your project, Clara. You're eleven now. These chickens are your first grown-up project, you think of them that way."

Is an eleven-year-old a grown-up? What would my father have thought of the grown-up project idea?

I do have a father. Everyone has a father. It's a law of nature. But I couldn't tell that to Tamar. *He doesn't exist,* she said. *You don't have a father.*

Chickens were not my idea. An animal of any kind would not have been my idea of a grown-up project. It's true that I wanted a grown-up project. It's true that I had complained to Tamar about not being given credit for no longer being a child. But chickens were not the answer I had envisioned.

"Tell me about my grandfather, and when you're done, tell me about my father," I said to Tamar a few months before the chickens arrived.

Hope springs eternal. It was my hope that if I occasionally, without warning, sprang the words—*grandfather, father*—on Tamar, she would be so startled that answers would spring unbidden to her lips.

"Nope and nope."

That was her response. That was a Tamarian answer.

"I'm an adult now," I said.

"You're eleven."

"In many cultures that would be considered nigh to adulthood."

"Nigh but no cigar," Tamar said.

She smiled. She liked the sound of that. I left her in the kitchen with a can of tomato soup and her can opener. I left her neither laughing nor chuckling. It could be said that when I left the kitchen after being told that I was nigh but no cigar, Tamar was *chortling*.

Three months later the chickens appeared.

In the beginning I tried to walk into the barn tall and stern, like I was in command. I carried the feed bucket in my left hand and the water bucket in my right, swinging them from side to side so that the water sloshed. Still, they attacked.

"Get off of me!" I yelled. "Get off of me, you devil-chickens!"

Then I tried to look like a man. I made my voice deep. I intoned.

*"Get the H away from me."*

Sometimes I even said the word. Get the HELL away. But

it didn't make any difference. The cocks just looked at me with their beady eyes and didn't move.

I named the meanest one CJ Wilson.

Why didn't I tell the old man about the real CJ Wilson either? I could have told him. He would have listened. You might think that I knew all the old man's secrets and he knew all mine. You would be wrong. Even now I wonder what secrets I never found out about the old man.

The first day of school last September, CJ Wilson corrected the teacher when she said his name at roll call: Charles Junior Wilson.

"It's CJ," he said. "Don't call me Charles Junior."

Winter comes right after Wilson.

"Clara Winter," said the teacher.

"It's Clara *winter*," I said.

"That's what I *said*."

She gave me a look. She was impatient. I could tell. After school CJ grabbed my leg as I walked past him on the school bus.

"Nice skirt," he said. "Nice skirt, Clara *Wipe*."

Then he flipped my skirt up so that my underwear showed. He hated me because Tamar is the Justice of the Peace of the Town of North Sterns and CJ's father had to come to her court at our house. Drunk driving.

"Good-bye and good riddance," Tamar said when CJ's father was gone. She was sitting at the kitchen table, which is her courtroom. Being JP is a part-time job. It takes about five hours a month to be JP of the Town of North Sterns. Tamar holds court wearing jeans and a T-shirt. She doesn't have a gavel. She says they're not essential.

"How are those chickens of yours?" she said.

"Fine."

"You getting any more eggs?"

"No."

There had only been a few that I could see, a few laid right by the gate so I could reach in quick and grab them.

"Well, look around good for them. That feed isn't free, you know."

"I know."

I couldn't even get near the pen. I stood four or five feet away, with the CJ Wilson chicken hissing from the dollhouse. I tossed the feed in a sudden jerk, aiming for the trough. The hens fought and gobbled for the bits of corn. While they were scrabbling I scooped up any eggs that I could see. Only one or two each time were close enough for me to grab through the bars. Where any others might be, I didn't know.

Laura Ingalls Wilder would not have feared my chickens.

Laura Ingalls Wilder was a snow lover. Laura was a true pioneer girl. Laura is the reason I call Tamar Ma to her face, because Ma is what pioneer girls called their mothers. I used to love Laura Ingalls Wilder when I was a child. When I started reading about Indians, I had to revise my initial impression of Laura. It was hard to do that. I loved Laura so much. At first I tried to defend her: it was way back then, they didn't know. Then I had to admit it: the pioneers were awful to the Indians.

"The pioneers were awful to the Indians," I said to the old man after we had become *compadres.*

"Yes," the old man said.

We were sitting at his kitchen table that had cigarette burn marks in it from the previous owner. The old man had found the kitchen table set out for the trash on scavenging night. I made some more toast. I spread it extremely thickly with margarine. I was embarrassed to have the old man see how much margarine I put on toast. I only did it when I was visiting him. He didn't seem to notice.

Tamar would never allow me to put so much margarine on toast. She has an eagle eye for that sort of thing.

"The problem is that I still love her," I said. "I love Laura."

"And what's the problem?"

"She was mean. She was awful to the Indians."

"An entire nation was awful to the Indians," he said. "They invaded their land, they pushed them onto reservations, they tried to kill them off."

"Yes. That's right. That's my point exactly."

"But still, you love her."

"Yes. That's my other point," I said. "My other exact point."

"It's the same point," he said.

I wrote that down. It had the ring of wisdom, although I didn't understand it. That used to happen to me when I was with the old man, not understanding something but knowing it was important. Being on the verge. That's how it felt. I used to write down the things he said. I kept track.

Are young chickens capable of hatred? Is it possible for an eleven-year-old girl to be killed by a flock of young chickens?

I would like to know.

I feel in my gut that the old man would have known what to do about my chickens. I should have told the old man about the chickens. There were things the old man knew that you would not have suspected he knew and chickens may well have been one of those things. After he was gone I researched chickens in the school library. Researching is one of my talents. There was nothing about a tendency toward violence in poultry. Feed, growth patterns, eggs, fryers versus roasters, and so on.

Violence? Nothing.

When CJ Wilson flipped my skirt up the first day of school he turned to the other boys and laughed. Some were embarrassed, some looked surprised. Some laughed along with CJ.

That's what happens when you're eleven. You say good-bye to the kids in your class in June, when school lets out. Maybe you'll see them a couple of times over the summer, maybe not. But in September, the day after Labor Day, you know you'll see them again. School will resume. Life will go on. You'll slide your tray through the cafeteria line: tiny fluted paper cups of applesauce, sloppy joe on hamburger buns. You know that nothing will have changed.

You're wrong.

You get on the bus the day after Labor Day and you're wearing new school clothes. New underwear, polka dot. CJ Wilson flips your skirt up and everything's changed. You never saw it coming.

# Chapter Three

The story of my birth is an astounding one. I was born during a February blizzard in a truck tipped sideways into a ditch on Glass Factory Road. My grandfather was trying to get Tamar to Utica Memorial in time for the delivery, but there was no such luck. Astonishingly, a midwife came walking by the stuck truck just at the critical moment.

The midwife was trying to get to Clearview Heights, the road on the hills above Utica where she lived with her husband and young child. She had to take Glass Factory, because it's the only road that intersects with Clearview Heights. The midwife, whose name was Angelica Rose Beaudoin, was driving her car and it broke down in the middle of that blizzard. Bravely, Angelica Rose laced her boots up and tied them into double knots. She rummaged in the back seat for the emergency road kit that her husband had put together for her in a recycled coffee can. In it, the young midwife found some chocolate bars, some change for a pay phone, extra mittens, a space blanket, and a pair of earmuffs. She put on the earmuffs. She wrapped the space blanket around her body, underneath her parka, for extra insulation. She put the extra pair of mittens on over the mittens she was already wearing.

I love thinking about Angelica Rose Beaudoin, the young midwife. Angelica Rose had not been a midwife for long. She had trained for emergency births but had not actually had to deliver a baby outside of the hospital or a home. Never in a blizzard.

Angelica Rose set off, keeping track of where she was by the telephone poles she could barely see through the driving snow. Up the steep hills and down she went, trudging her way toward Clearview Heights and home. Darkness was all about her, and the snow felt like stinging bees on her face. Her feet made no sound in the powdery snow. Unbeknownst to the snow, or to the frozen ground beneath it, the young midwife was thinking about a baby, her own baby, who had been born without ears. Within his tiny skull, Angelica Rose's child had the means of hearing, but with no passage to the outside world her son lived in an unknown world. Sound came to him as if from underwater. His mother's voice floated past his round baby-fuzzed head as if in a bubble. What her baby heard was not what was heard by her. What her baby heard was his own, his own to make sense of, his own to understand. Already, his mother could see a difference in the way her child inclined his head to speech.

Angelica Rose trudged through the snow and thought about things that were missing, things that were broken and could not be fixed.

Then, from the heart of the blizzard, the midwife heard a muffled cry.

Angelica Rose cocked her head and listened again, to make sure she wasn't imagining it. The cry came again.

*Help!*

It was my grandfather, calling for help through a hairline crack in the driver's side window. He didn't want to leave my mother and search for help, but hoping against hope that someone would pass by, he kept calling out the window into the storm. *Heeeeeeeelp,* he called, once every couple of minutes, while Tamar twisted in the seat next to him.

"Helloooooo!"

That was the sound of the midwife's voice, responding to the person in need. My grandfather heard her voice. Disbelieving, he cranked open the window, struggled out into the snow and found the midwife, her head turning this way and that, listening for that lone cry of help.

"Come on! My daughter's having a baby!"

That was what my grandfather said. Angelica Rose Beaudoin said not another word. She had been trained for this moment. She nodded, started beating her mittened hands together to warm them, and followed my grandfather to the truck in the ditch. As she stumbled after him she summoned all her medical training and ordered her mind as to what needed to be done. They found Tamar in agony on the front seat.

The midwife pushed her way in and cradled Tamar's head. She spoke soothingly and quietly to Tamar, to calm Tamar's fears and prepare her for what was to happen.

The old man listened carefully to the story. Already he knew of my fear and loathing of snow and cold. Blizzards especially. I could tell the old man was listening carefully because the more carefully he listened, the more he tilted his head. His head was semihorizontal. That used to happen sometimes, when I was telling a story and the old man was listening.

"And then my twin sister was born, and I was next," I said. "And that's the story in a nutshell. That's all she wrote."

"You have a twin sister?" the old man said.

"Indeed I do."

"Does she live with you?"

"She lives with me in a way," I said. "In a certain manner of speaking, she lives with me."

"In a certain manner of speaking?"

"In a sense," I said. "In a sense my twin sister lives with me."

He looked at me.

"Do you want me to heat some more water for coffee?" I asked.

"All right," the old man said.

I got up and filled the old man's teakettle with water and put it on to boil. I looked out the window over the old man's kitchen sink toward the Twin Churches. An hour had already gone by. Tamar and the choir would be winding down in another forty-five minutes.

Often I have wondered about Angelica Rose Beaudoin, where she is now, if she ever remembers me and my baby sister. Angelica Rose was extremely grateful that her husband had thought to put earmuffs into the emergency blizzard road kit, because she had only a hat that didn't cover her ears. You have to be vigilant about exposed extremities in an upstate New York blizzard. Extremities are the first to go.

And what became of her child, her hearing but uneared child? I wonder about that too.

I brought the old man more coffee.

"Where is she?"

"Who? Angelica Rose Beaudoin?"

"No. Your twin sister."

"I only wish I knew," I said.

My baby sister is the reason why I hate my last name. It's a name of cold and ice and snow. People who look at me see a girl named Clara Winter. They don't ever think about the significance of my last name, and if they do, they see a world of whiteness. Blowing snow, drifting fields of white. Maybe some of them see the darkness of trees, winter branches reaching into an empty sky. Maybe others picture the Adirondacks in January, the green of evergreens so dark that it could be mistaken for black.

I spell my last name with a lowercase w, but I'm the only one who knows that a lowercase w is a rejection of winter, an acknowledgment of what winter really is and how it can kill.

"What do you mean?" the old man said. He gazed at me with his head nearly horizontal. "You said that she lives with you."

"What I mean is that the entire story I just told you is a lie," I said.

The old man took a drink of coffee, which he drank only after it was almost cold. He looked at me. I looked at him. Words hung in the air between us, heavy and dark. We sat that way until Tamar drove up and honked her secret Tamar honk, two shorts and an extralong: *beep-beep, beeeeeeeeeeeeeeeep.*

I dreamed about the old man that night. It was silent. Lights flickered. People I didn't know were coming through the woods from far away bringing lights that were lanterns, lanterns for the old man.

I woke up and thought, I may not be a metalworker but I can still make lanterns. I could bring lanterns for the old man.

Why not? I went down to the closet in the kitchen where we hang the can bag. It's a plastic Jewell's Grocery bag and we throw tin cans into it. It was the middle of the night. I didn't want to wake Tamar so I used the flashlight that I keep under my bed in case of emergency. But the bag came tumbling down and all the cans spilled and Tamar came rushing down the stairs holding her baseball bat with both hands.

"What the hell's going on, Clara?"

"I was getting a snack," I lied. "Then I bumped into the closet and all the cans spilled."

She thunked her baseball bat on the floor a few times.

"I'm sorry," I said.

"Pick up this mess and go back to bed," she said. "You've got school tomorrow and your chickens to feed beforehand."

I picked them all up. Next morning after Tamar was gone, before the bus came, and after I fed my chickens I cleaned out the biggest cans, the ones that Italian plum tomatoes come in. Plum tomato cans don't need much washing. A swish or two and they're done. No grease, that's why.

I was determined to make lanterns for the old man. It was a semifixation. That's what Tamar would have called it, had she known about my desire.

"Another semifixation on the part of my daughter," she would have said.

Tamar often talks that way, as if someone else is in the kitchen. In real life Tamar puts on and scrapes off huge orange flower decals on Dairylea milk trucks on an as-needed basis. Decals are always needed, though, so Tamar's job is full-time. She leans extension ladders against the sides of the milk tank trucks and climbs up to the top and scrapes and peels all day long. In winter she scrapes and peels inside a giant semi-heated milk truck garage in Utica. They assign Tamar to the decal work because she doesn't mind heights. She's fearless. She's known for it. The JP job is a sideline. Speeding, drunk driving, boundary disputes: these are the usual cases. The oldest Miller boy, for growing marijuana in the middle of his father's biggest cornfield.

Once in a while there's a wedding.

The old man used to make lanterns when he was a child, in his country that he would not tell me the name of because he said it didn't exist anymore. I am older than the old man was when he learned the art of metalworking. If he could do it, so can I, I thought.

It was hard work, puncturing the sides of those tomato cans. The church key didn't want to do a good job. A few of the cans buckled under the pressure. I strung twine through the holes to hang the lanterns by. After school I bought some burgundy-colored votive candles at Jewell's from the reject bin.

"Burgundy votive candles," Mr. Jewell said. "An unusual item for an unusual girl."

He smiled at me.

"And what do you plan to do with these burgundy votive candles?" he asked. "Or is that a secret?"

"Secret."

"I thought as much. Would you care for a Persian, Miss Winter?"

I could hear the capital W in the way he said my name. No one but me knows it's lowercase. He reached for the box of Persians that he and his friend Spooner Hughes were eating from. "Fresh," he said. "Made them myself."

"Thank you."

The secret to a good Persian doughnut is extra glaze. Also, they double the amount of cinnamon. Mr. Jewell told me that once.

I hung the plum tomato can lanterns in the old man's weeping willow tree. It's hard to hang can lanterns in a weeping willow. The branches bend. With a scratching sound, they scrape across the top of hard shiny snow, old snow, the kind of snow you find in the middle of a cold snap in March. I had to choose the thickest branches of the weeping willow; otherwise the lanterns dragged the branches down too far and made the tree look sad.

It was going to be a surprise for the old man. I knew he wasn't in the trailer because I had stood on the cinder block outside the little window by the built-in bed and seen that he was not there. Also, I had jumped up and down at the curved end of the trailer and seen that he was not sitting in his tiny curved-wall kitchen.

Each can that I hung I put a lighted burgundy votive candle into. I didn't hang them too high. I was only eleven. I wasn't that tall.

The can lanterns swung in the branches of the weeping willow tree.

The neighbor lady from the greenish trailer three trailers down from the old man's opened her door. She had a scarf tied around her head. She was leaning out her door with slippers on. I could see her mouth moving but I closed my ears to the sound of her voice. Then she came out with a pair of big boots on. They were not tied. They were men's.

The sound of the neighbor lady's voice seeped in anyway.

"Miss? What, may I ask, are you doing?"

"It's a surprise for the old man."

"You mean George?"

You could hear that she didn't know his real name. *Georg*.

"Old tomato cans hung in his tree?" she said. "That's your surprise?"

"It's a secret. You won't get the full visual effect until nightfall," I said. "Then you'll see."

She raised her eyebrows. Then she backed into her trailer and shut the door. Finally they were all hung. Where was the old man? He could have walked into Sterns. It was only one-quarter of a mile, which is not a far distance. He could have been doing his shopping at Jewell's. He went there once a week and always bought the same things: elbow macaroni, spaghetti sauce, three cans of tuna, one quart of milk, canned peaches in heavy syrup, a package of Fig Newtons, two loaves of bread, one container of whipped margarine, and two boxes of frozen peas. That used to last him a week, even with me there on Wednesday nights, eating toast.

Sometimes he put tuna in his spaghetti sauce before he poured it over his bowl of elbow macaroni. I saw him do that on a semiregular basis.

Tamar was at choir practice. The stained-glass windows all lit up. It was pitch dark when I finished tying all the cans into the tree.

Still no old man.

The neighbor lady stuck her head out the door again and watched me for a few minutes. She didn't say anything. I walked around the trailer park three times. There's a road that goes around the whole thing. Around and around I went, so my feet wouldn't freeze. Keep stamping and walking, that's the way to keep the circulation going. When the feet of the pioneers froze they stripped off their boots and socks and rubbed them with snow in front of a roaring fire. It was extremely painful. The pioneers lost fingers and toes.

Winter kills.

The third time I walked around the trailer park road I came upon the cans in the weeping willow and they looked different. Things change. You think they won't. You don't plan on things ever changing, but then you take a walk around a trailer park and you come back around, and things are different. You've moved into the future, even a little bit, and things don't look the same.

I saw that the cans were not lanterns. I did not have the skill of the old man. I could not work with metal; I could not make something beautiful out of a plum tomato can. I had not yet become the old man's apprentice. My lanterns were just old tomato cans, stuck in a tree whose branches were too spindly to support them. It took me only a few minutes to cut them all down with the Swiss army knife I carry in case of emergency. When I turned around, there was the old man, watching, standing there with a plastic Jewell's bag hanging from each hand.

"I brought you a sugar cookie from Jewell's," he said. "It's the kind of sugar cookie I ate when I was a child."

"In your country that doesn't exist anymore?" I said.

"That's right."

The old man did not say, What were you doing, stringing plum tomato cans in a tree? That was the difference between the old man and Tamar. She would have said, What the hell are you up to now, Clara Winter? She would have said, I have a strange child.

The old man was late that night because he wanted to offer me a treat. He wanted to have a sugar cookie waiting for me when I came to visit him. He didn't say that, but I could tell. That's what I believe to be true.

"When we got to Ellis Island, they almost wouldn't let me in," the old man said one night after we had become *compadres*.

"Why not?"

"Retarded. They thought I was retarded."

"But you weren't."

I tried to picture the old man as a kid. A skinny boy body floated into my mind. A skinny boy body with an old man's face.

"Why would they think you were special ed if you weren't?"

"My nose," he said. "I used to draw in the air with my nose. If you look down the corners of your eyes you can see the outline of your nose. Pretend that the end of it is a pen. Draw something in the air."

"Noses don't draw," I said. "Noses can run but they can't draw. Ha! Get it?"

I tried it. He was right. My nose made a nice invisible line. C, L, A, R, A. I wrote my name in invisible capital letters. Then I wrote my last name: w, i, n, t, e, r.

"I was tracing the outline of the American flag on Ellis Island," the old man said. "With my nose. That's why they thought I was retarded."

"Tell me about your family of origin," I said.

That's a term they told us to use in the oral histories. Your family of origin is the one you started out with.

"Georg, who is myself."

I knew the first time I heard his name to leave the "e" off. It's one of my skills. Clara Winter, you have an inborn sense of spelling, my fifth-grade teacher told me.

"My parents. Eli, my young brother."

"Do you have relatives back where you came from?"

"Where I came from does not exist," the old man said. "It used to be one country. Now it's another country."

"But there's got to be people related to you there."

"I am the last of my line."

That was one sentence that I wrote down in its entirety: *I am the last of my line.* It had the ring of truth.

"Tell me about being an immigrant," I said to the old man. "Tell me about leaving your country."

It's my belief that the old man could be called a pioneer.

"I held the lantern," the old man said. "That was my job."

I wrote it down.

"It was dark. I held it pointed in back of me so that my brother Eli could see his way. If I didn't look at the light from the lantern, the moon was light enough for me. You can't let your eyes get used to an abundance of light, that's the trick."

*An abundance of light.*

My roll of green adding-machine paper kept spooling out. It didn't seem to matter to him. That was the secret with the old man: get him talking and keep him going. That was how I discovered the nuances of his life.

"So I got to Ellis Island," he said.

"And what then?"

You had to keep him talking when he started, otherwise all was lost.

"And then nothing," he said. "It was all over then, the woods and the lantern and the walking. I lost two toes. They almost didn't let me in because of the nose-writing. They thought I was retarded."

"Special ed," I said.

"Retarded."

"And then what?"

"And then I started work. Metalwork. I am a metalworker."

That was something I knew. He didn't know that for two hours on a March night, a girl of eleven had spied on him through a piece of patched glass, had watched him hang lantern after lantern in the trees. I said nothing.

He stirred his coffee until it slopped into his saucer. I spread some more margarine on my one last bite of toast. I didn't want him to see how thick I was spreading it so I held it beneath the rim of the table. I was getting addicted to thickly spread margarine. There's something about the taste. It's cool. It slides around your mouth.

"Did your brother write with his nose, too? Did the Ellis Island guys think he was retarded, too?"

But the old man was done talking. *Finis.* I could tell. I could always tell, with the old man. He stirred his coffee until it slopped into the saucer, and then I drank my hot chocolate and ate my toast and he waited until his coffee was cold and then he drank it, and then we sat until the clock said I had six minutes. It was time for me to go. Tamar would be driving up to the curb by the Nine Mile Trailer Park sign in exactly six minutes. That's how long it took her to get from choir practice to the trailer park, including saying good-bye to her friends and starting the car. Tamar is never late.

"Bye," I said.

He didn't say good-bye. I knew he wouldn't. He was in his dark lantern world. I shut the door tight behind me so the snow wouldn't drift inside and make a tiny pile by his door, like sawdust. Tamar drove up on the dot, eating a miniature ice cream sandwich from the front freezer case at Jewell's. Even in the dead of winter she loves them. They're only a quarter each.

# Chapter Four

I used to wonder why my chickens turned mean. Lack of sunshine, maybe. The corner of the broken-down barn where Tamar built the pen was dark. No windows. It was a big pen but nothing in it was interesting, not even my old doll-house, the rusty one that the younger Miller boys wrecked years ago when they held their Final Battle of the G.I. Joes.

One day the January after I got the chickens, I went in with the feed and water. It was hard to see at first because the snow was so bright outside, the barn so dark inside. The CJ Wilson chicken was sitting in the dollhouse. Right in the living room where the winning G.I. Joe busted through the floor. He stared at me. He didn't blink his nasty beady eyes.

See, he was saying to me. This is my house. There are my women.

I looked in the corner and saw the other cock lying dead. Pecked to death by the CJ Wilson chicken. I took the barn shovel and scooped up the carcass, carried it out to the pasture and flung it into the weeds. Then I went back into the house, washed my hands, scraped the bottoms of my boots, and got on the bus when Tiny pulled up to the driveway.

That was the first day that I knew I was in for a long haul with my chickens. Next to the chicken problem, the real CJ Wilson momentarily faded in importance. When he got on the bus there must have been a look on my face because he said not a word, just pointed out the window as Tiny pulled away from his trailer.

"You see that car?" said CJ to the North Sterns boys. "You see it?"

An old white Camaro with rust spots was parked in a snowdrift in CJ's unplowed driveway.

"Yeah," said one of the boys.

"That's mine," said CJ. "My dad, he's saving that for me. For when I get my license. He's going to fix it up and give it to me on my sixteenth birthday."

The boys nodded.

"It's a Camaro. He's saving it for me. Hey, Wipe! Your chickenshit mother got a car for you?"

I said nothing. I never said anything to CJ.

"Didn't think so," CJ said.

Occasionally I used to think about writing a fake book report about a boy named, for example, CJ Wilson. In the morning, when the chickens squawked and pecked, when I brought them their food and water in two buckets, with the snow packing down into my boots, I thought about CJ. I thought about the fake book report I could write about CJ, disguising his name to protect the innocent although he isn't innocent.

But I've never written a word.

"My dad used to be a professional wrestler," CJ said on the bus one day. "His name was Chucky Luck. He had his own show on TV."

CJ screwed his mouth up and squinted his eyes, punching his arms straight ahead of him like pistons. Grunting like a pig.

"Yeah right!" said one of the boys. "How come I never heard of it?"

"Before you were born, asshole," said CJ. "He doesn't do it anymore."

"Well if it was before I was born Tiny must have seen it. Tiny, you seen it?" asked the boy.

Tiny shoved down another handful of M&Ms and laughed the way he does, which sounds like a cough.

"See?" said CJ. "Tiny's heard of Chucky Luck."

All those boys live out on the border of North Sterns. Sometimes they used to yell to me.

"Come sit by your boyfriend, Clara," they yelled. "Come sit on CJ's lap."

The first time they did that I didn't get off at my stop. Tiny went right on by when I didn't come lurching up the aisle to wait by the door. I sank down in my seat and peered over the bottom of the window, watching the boys get off. Each one at his own trailer. The bus dropped off its last passenger, Bonita Rae Farwell, and turned around in Ray Farwell's rutted pasture-track. Tiny squinted in his rearview mirror. He reached into his M&M bag and tossed down another handful.

"What in the H you doing back there, Clara Winter?"

"I'm sorry, Tiny. I forgot to get off."

"Well what were you thinking, Clara?"

"I don't know. I guess I was reading and I missed the stop."

"Now I gotta go back all the way to North Sterns to let you off. We all know you got a brain in that head of yours, little girl, you use it now."

"I'm sorry, Tiny."

Tiny revved the engine so I could feel it throb under my feet. I watched Tiny's hand go back and forth from the bag to his mouth. When I got off he smiled at me. Little pointy black teeth.

You would not have known it to look at him, but the old man was a hero. In his life, he was a savior of babies, treed cats, and victims of natural disaster. In large and small ways and always for the better, the old man changed the lives of those who encountered him. I used to sit across from the old man at his cigarette-burned kitchen table and picture him as a young man, doing his heroic deeds.

The old man, as a young man, once saved a baby from drowning. Back where the old man came from, in his country that doesn't exist anymore, natural disasters were not a rarity. Spring floods, winter storms, summer tornadoes: these were the realities of the old-man-as-a-young-man's life.

Once, when the old man was only eleven, a spring flood came that was worse than the village had ever known. Flood legends that went back hundreds of years in the life of the village did not begin to match the enormity of what the old man and the villagers were seeing. The dikes, which were constructed of flower-patterned flour sacks stuffed with sand, gave way. Angry gray water foaming with yellow spume and filled with debris and broken dishes spewed over the top of the banks and exploded through the streets of the town.

"Georg! Climb to the roof!"

That was Georg's mother calling to him, frantic that her son be safe in the face of the water that threatened to overtake him. Georg, heeding his mother's cry, swiftly climbed the wooden peg ladder that leaned against the loft of the hut in which he lived with his parents.

"Where is Papa?" he shouted to his mother as he climbed.

"Still in the forge!" his mother called back.

Clutching her apron filled with the family's most treasured possessions—a Bible, three silver forks, the white baby dress that Georg, and later his brother Eli had been christened in—Georg's mother climbed after him. Together they huddled on the thatched roof of their cottage, holding hands and silently praying.

Remember, the old man was only eleven.

The roar of the water drowned out almost all other sound. For hours Georg and his mother crouched on the thatch, made slippery by the rain that accompanied the flood. The sky was dark and heavy with water. All around them the people of the village, neighbors they had known all their lives, huddled on their own roofs. On one, an old woman had managed to shove her pig through a hole in the thatch. She tethered him to the chimney with a rope and knelt next to him as he squealed and tried to push away the leash with his snout.

"Where, is, Papa?" Georg called again. Even though his mother was next to him, holding his hand, he had to yell because the noise of the thunder and rain and racing water drowned out sound.

His mother looked at him and said nothing. She shook her head.

"Pray," she said.

Then Georg's sharp ears heard a cry that was not of the wind or water. So faintly that he could not be sure he'd actually heard it, the cry of a newborn came drifting past. Borne on the wind of the storm, the cry was gone almost before it came. In the next moment it came again, and then again.

*There's a baby out there,* Georg thought.

He looked at his mother, her eyes closed tight against the driving rain and the tears that were blinding her. Across the street now filled by raging floodwaters, the old woman had put her arms around her pig and was holding it as if it were a child. The infant's cry came again, and young Georg felt his heart contract. He crouched and scanned the surrounding huts. *Where was the child?* The cry came again, and it was then that he saw her. Wrapped in a yellow blanket, placed in the forked limb of a black locust tree, as if someone in great haste had tried to do the one thing she could think of to save her child. Georg knew that it was up to him and him alone to bring the child to safety. Who else was there? Who else had heard the child's cry?

His mother had buried her head in her hands by then. Unseeing, unhearing, she was lost in a chanted prayer for Georg's father, still at the forge.

Quickly, before he lost his courage, Georg scrambled back into the loft and then down the peg ladder into the kitchen. Water had reached the halfway mark of the wall, and Georg lost his footing. Before he was swept under and out the door, he managed to take off his boots and soaked tunic. Then he was in the water, and part of the flood.

Getting across the street, which had become a torrent of water and debris, took many minutes. Every time he was swept under the surface of the frantic water, Georg held his breath and struggled to find his footing, struggled to the top again, gasped in a great lungful of air and shook the water from his eyes.

The baby cried, and cried again. Led by the thin wail of the baby's fear and sorrow, Georg found himself at the scarred trunk of the black locust, fighting to stay upright. Above him the faded yellow of the blanket hung suspended in the crotch of the tree. A tattered corner dangled in front of his reaching fingertips. The baby's cry was the cry of all babies, lost and alone and bereft. *If I could just reach that baby, if I could just—*

Do you see how it happens? Can you feel it growing inside your own heart? An old man tilts his shoulder in a certain way, or rubs his eye, and then it all comes over you. The yellow blanket, the raging floodwaters, a boy's mother crouched on a thatched roof crying for her lost husband. It all comes tumbling out.

The real story of my birth is that there was no midwife.

Angelica Rose Beaudoin, American Midwife, never lived or breathed. She never delivered two twin girls in a truck in the ditch in the middle of winter. She never stayed with my grandfather and Tamar, sharing her chocolate bars and telling jokes and stories, making sure Tamar was resting and recovering and not bleeding to death, until the Glass Factory Road snowplow came through. It never happened.

There was only Tamar and my grandfather and me: me crying, Tamar half-passed-out and bleeding, my grandfather not knowing what to do with my baby sister who lay wrapped in a scrap of blanket on the seat between them.

That's what I see when I think of the story of my birth. That's why I prefer to think about Angelica Rose Beaudoin, the brave young midwife.

Had there been an Angelica Rose Beaudoin, she would have seen immediately what the problem was. A trained midwife would have known what to do. She would have breathed life into my sister, rubbed her tiny chest, warmed her until she was a living being. The midwife would have stripped off the space blanket her husband had packed for her in the recycled coffee can emergency road kit, wrapped my sister up in it and handed her to my grandfather, who would have cradled her and rocked her.

Then I would have been born. I would have been strong and healthy, screaming from the first. *A healthy baby girl*, the midwife would have said to Tamar. *Two healthy baby girls.* A story with a happy ending, the kind of sixth-grade fake book report that my teachers would give me an A on.

It was the dead of winter, a February blizzard. Tamar couldn't get to the hospital, that was the whole problem. Her father was driving her in his truck. This was in the days before four-wheel drive. That's what Tamar said the one time I heard her talking to the choir director about it on the phone. She said, "Now there's four-wheel drive. That would have made all the difference." She had me and my twin sister in a ditch halfway to the hospital in Utica. Tamar couldn't hold us in. When babies want to be born they will be born. Nothing can stop them.

"We were born before four-wheel drive," I said.

The old man nodded.

"The problem is that they never should have taken Glass Factory," I said. "In a blizzard you never take Glass Factory. You take Route 12. You get to the hospital sooner. You don't wait until the last minute. You don't take Glass Factory hoping to save half a mile, hoping that some midwife will just happen to be passing by in the middle of a blizzard."

I had a twin sister. I think about her all the time.

If she were alive, people would talk about us in a different way. It would be "Tamar and her girls," "Miss Winter and the twins," "Tamar Winter and her daughters." Tamar refused to name my sister when she was born dead. Bad luck, she said. But what I believe to be true is that all babies should have a name. When I think about my sister, there is no name attached to my thoughts. She is nameless. All I see in my mind is _____, which I have changed to Baby Girl.

Tamar never told me about my sister. If it had not been for the choir director, I would still be living my life knowing that something was missing but not knowing that something was my twin sister.

"Your mother has a beautiful voice," the choir director said to me when I was nine years old, before I met the old man, when I used to have to sit in the sanctuary listening to the choir practice.

"Do you have a beautiful voice, too?" she asked me.

"Mediocre," I said, which is true.

"Imagine if you had a beautiful voice and your poor dead twin had had a beautiful voice," the choir director said. "The Twin Churches would have soared with the angelic voices of the three Winter women."

That's how the choir director talks.

"That poor baby," the choir director said. "She never had a chance, did she?"

I shook my head. I said nothing. I waited for more, but none was forthcoming. Even though I was only nine at the time and Tamar had never mentioned a word, I knew that what the choir director said was true. I had a twin. I could feel it in my bones.

My baby sister was dead, my chickens wanted to kill me, and the old man came from a country that doesn't exist anymore. Those were the kinds of secrets that I used to write down on my spool of green adding-machine paper, on Wednesday night when I visited the old man in his trailer. Soon I had unspooled enough paper to make several curls. Enough to hang to the floor.

I wish now that I had told the old man about CJ Wilson and the other boys and Tiny and the chickens. I wish that one cold night when my chickens were just beginning to be mean, and Tamar was at choir practice, and I had made the old man his coffee and me my hot chocolate, and we were sitting at his kitchen table and I was eating my toast spread with an inordinate amount of margarine and he was stirring his coffee with the handle of his spoon, I had told the old man everything.

Tamar says I'm crazy. Tamar says, That baby was dead before she was born. Tamar says, Give up.

But my sister was alive before she was dead, wasn't she? She grew the same as me, swimming around in a little water world. We knew each other. We touched each other. We would have been together forever.

Winter killed my baby sister. Not only was she my twin sister; she was my identical twin. I can feel that in my bones, too. If it hadn't been a blizzard, and if the truck hadn't gone off the road into the ditch, and if the plow hadn't chosen to do Route 12 before Glass Factory Road, my mother, Tamar, and my grandfather would have gotten to the hospital on time and my twin sister and I would have been born in the hospital and my sister would have lived. This is what I believe to be true.

"My mother didn't name my sister," I told the old man after we were *compadres.* "She did not give her own child a name. Is that even a possibility?"

"Anything's a possibility," the old man said.

"But she buried her," I said. "You don't bury someone unless you think of her as someone. If she was someone enough to bury, she was someone enough to have a name."

"You don't know what was going through your mother's head."

"But her own child?"

"She was not *your* child, she was your sister," the old man said. "There's a difference."

My sister is stuck forever at the spot where she was born. She was born there and she died there, while I lived and grew. I'm still growing. There's no telling how tall I'll be when all's said and done.

Tamar doesn't have the memory to connect her September blue sky and the smell of autumn leaves with the coming snow and what it means. She pushes it out of her mind. She pretends there never was another baby. She pretends that I was the only one. You don't have a sister, she says, stop dragging her into conversation all the time.

"But what would you have named her?" I used to ask her.

I can't help it. I've got to know.

"I wouldn't have named her anything," Tamar says. "She was born *dead*. And that's the end of it."

"But what if?" I say. "What if? Just tell me. Just give her a name."

She doesn't answer. She never answers. She has condemned me forever to think of my sister as Blank.

"She wasn't ever alive!" Tamar says. "Get it through your head, Clara. *You never had a sister.*"

I did, though. She swam beside me for nine months. We might have held hands inside Tamar's womb. Our noses might have touched. She might have played a game with me, pushing me around with her tiny unborn foot.

If you have seen a death certificate, you know what a small piece of paper it is. If you have ever searched your mother's bureau drawer for something that would be proof of your twin sister's existence, you might have been surprised at how small and simple a death certificate is. You don't even have to put someone's name down on a death certificate. If the person who died was a baby, all you have to put is "Baby" and the baby's last name. For example, "Baby Girl Winter."

If only the snow hadn't been blowing horizontally the way it does in an upstate New York blizzard, if my grandfather had only been able to rock his truck out of the ditch. If only Tamar hadn't mistaken early labor pains for indigestion and started for Utica sooner, if only we had just managed to stay inside her belly instead of forcing our way out. If only Angelica Rose Beaudoin, American Midwife, had been a real person.

But that's a different story. That's the story I would have written myself: my twin sister and I alive together, each the other's half, one child under God indivisiblewithlibertyand-justiceforall. That's the kind of book report I would have written, if I had made up a book about me and my sister.

"I want my sister," I said. "I want Baby Girl Winter."

The old man said nothing. He got up and carried his coffee cup and the plate that my sugar cookie had been on to his miniature sink. He put the stopper in and squeezed one small squirt of dish soap into the sink, then ran hot water. I watched him do that the exact same way every single time I ever visited the old man.

# Chapter Five

What sorts of books are placed by garbage cans on garbage night in the town of Sterns? Mainly they're old class books, the kind people carry around in boxes in their basements for twenty years and then one day think: *I will never again in my entire life open this book and there is no sense in its taking up valuable space in my basement,* and they throw them out. Right out by the garbage cans they put them, in cardboard boxes with the bottoms falling out.

Books should not ever be treated that way. It's a sin to treat a book that way. That's what I believe to be true.

The world of my childhood is behind me now. I am no longer a child and I have put away childish things. But childish things come back to haunt you. The destruction of books is something I would not have visited upon even my most hated enemy. Had you asked me, I would have termed myself incapable of such an act.

There it is, though: I was a book ripper.

It hurts me now to think about it. I can't remember the actual ripping as I was only a baby. At most, a very small child.

Tamar told me about it on a day when I came to her holding a library book that someone had written in in purple magic marker. Not only that, but the top corner of each page had been creased, folded over in a triangle as if every page was a book-mark. It had to be the same magic marker person. A maniac.

"How can someone do this?" I said to Tamar.

She was making split pea soup, the only item of food that she actually cooks from scratch. A soup I like to eat but hate the smell of while it's cooking.

"Ma? Look."

I showed her the book, each page corner worn and creased, purple magic marker underlining certain paragraphs.

"And the thing is, the paragraphs that this person under-lined don't even stand out," I said. "There's not one thing spe-cial about any of these underlined paragraphs."

Tamar took a cursory look. How I love that word. There may not be anyone in the world who loves the word *cursory* as much as I do. That's how I am about certain words.

"See what I mean?"

"Doesn't look so bad to me," she said. "Considering how you used to rip books to pieces when you were a baby."

She dumped two cupfuls of tiny hard green peas into the giant pot she makes soup in. They sank to the bottom with a clattering sound. Immediately the boiling water in the pot stopped boiling. It settled down and became ferociously quiet, working hard to start boiling again. The quietness of the once-boiling water made it seem as if the water was too busy to make noise. *I mean business* is what is meant by that absence of sound.

"What are you talking about?" I said.

"You," she said. "Clara Winter, defender of books. You used to rip them to shreds. Drove me crazy."

The water in the pot began to hum in a sinister way. A low, gathering hum, bringing itself back to a boil as if getting ready to go off to war.

"Any kind of book," she said. "Your baby books, my books, books belonging to other people. You'd rip the cover to pieces, then you'd start on the insides. You were possessed."

She took a bite of honey toast, a big one right out of the folded-over middle. That's something about Tamar. She greatly prefers the soft middle of bread, but she would not admit it, nor would she ever not eat her crusts. On her deathbed, Tamar will be finishing her crusts. That's the kind of person she is.

"Little Clara rips books, I scream at little Clara, little Clara laughs," Tamar said. "That's the way it was."

I had my roll of green note-taking adding-machine paper ready in its paper holder. The old man made the paper holder out of tin for me. He followed directions by looking at the pictures in his book *Metalworking Made Easy*. It holds my roll of adding-machine paper perfectly. It keeps it taut and tight, ready for me to take notes on.

"Yup," Tamar said. "That's all she wrote."

*That's all*, I wrote.

Books? Books are sacred. Books are to me what the host is to the priest, the oasis to the desert wanderer, the arrival of winged seraphim to a dying man. That's the main reason why I can't write a book report. I can't stand what a book report does, boils a book down to a few sentences about plot. What about the words that make each book unique, an island unto itself, words like *cursory* and *ingenuous* and *immerse*? What about the *heart and soul*?

Plot? Who cares?

My plots are always interesting. They're just not real. After the last report I wrote, my teacher sent me a personal note: "Clara, you have an intuitive understanding of how to include just enough information about a book to make your report exciting, while not giving away the ending. I am intrigued now and I may just have to go read this book myself."

That's the danger. She wants to know the nonexistent ending to a nonexistent book. I know how she feels. After I finish making up a book report, I myself want to read the book. I myself feel as if the book is out there, searching for me, with an ending I don't know, a future waiting to be written.

The old man knew of my love of books. He used to gather them for me on scavenging nights. Another place to get books is garage sales, of which there are many in a Sterns summer, but the old man didn't do that. He didn't go places where there might be crowds of people. He was a loner, the old man. He preferred solitude to conviviality.

*Conviviality.* Six syllables. A word that would be hard to say were English not your mother tongue.

Some of the books the old man gathered for me were not to my taste. I said nothing, though. He chose them mostly for their pictures and photos. I could tell. They had personal meaning for him, the books that he chose. I always thanked the old man when he saved a book for me. Here's the kind of book that appealed to him: *Metalworking Made Easy,* by William J. Becker. 1942. The old man had *Metalworking Made Easy* open to the page that showed a picture of how to make a tin paper roller.

"This would be useful for you," the old man said. "You could put your roll of adding-machine paper in it and it would keep it taut."

That was thoughtful of him, to think of me and my adding-machine paper. Next time I came to visit, he had a paper roller waiting for me. He had made it out of some sheet metal that he cut with his tin snips and soldered together with his solder iron. It looked just like the one in the book.

If you know how to read, you know how forever. You can't unread. You can't ever look at a word and not know what that word is, precisely and permanently. You just can't do it. They should tell you that when you're a kid, that once you get into phonics you're into them for life.

"There's no backing out, kiddo," they should say.

Brainwashing. That's what it actually is.

The old man though, he was a different matter. The old man was seventy-seven years old. When I met him, he was exactly seven times as old as me. How I love numbers that are multiples of eleven. They are far more interesting than multiples of ten, which are what the structure of the world revolves around when you think about it.

Here's a secret about the old man: he did not know how to read.

A few months after I met the old man I had a dream. I was on Ellis Island. The old man was standing on the edge of a pier. He was wearing a coat with a round collar like in the olden days. He was a boy. He was seventeen years old. His nose was moving, lines and stars and rectangles. The shape of the American flag.

The old man had told me that he used to use the tip of his nose to write in the air as a child. He called it air-writing. In my dream, there was a certain look in the old-man-as-a-young-man's eyes. I woke up and I knew he couldn't read.

I proved it.

"I'm writing you a message in the air with my nose," I said.

This was one day after he told me about the air-writing.

"You see if you can figure it out," I said.

I wrote it in small letters: *bye.* That was the whole message, three small letters. It was time for me to go. Tamar didn't like to drive all the way in to the old man's trailer. She liked me to walk out to the entrance and meet her there. It's good for you, Clara, she used to say, the fresh air.

"Good," he said, after I wrote it in the air with my nose. "You're getting the hang of it."

"What did it say?" I said. "Did you really figure it out?"

"I did."

"But could you tell I was writing *bye?*"

"I could."

*Nay sir, I think not.*

I tested him again.

I wrote him a note and put it under his coffee cup when I brought it over to the table.

"What's this?" he said.

He pulled it out and looked at it.

"What do you think?" I said.

"Very good."

Why did I have to test him again? There wasn't any need to. How I wish I hadn't written what I wrote on that note: *I know you can't read.*

• • •

The old man remembered things in colors and sounds, not letters. Shapes he could hold in his head, and ideas, and memory was locked in him tighter than you can imagine. He had learned to form the words of his name. I watched him do it on the check he used to get every month. He made the letters by putting slashes here and slashes there: Georg Kominsky. You could tell he didn't know how to make real letters. Letters to the old man were only shapes and sticks and curves, actors strutting and fretting on a stage, signifying nothing.

Picture all that came into the old man's life that he never knew the meaning of: words and sentences and paragraphs and pages. Pages and pages and pages.

How many letters came to his trailer, and to all the places he may have lived before the trailer? How many people in this world sat down once late at night, lit a candle or turned on a lamp, and took pen in hand to write to the old man?

*Dear Georg.*

*Dearest Georg.*

*My beloved Georg.*

And nothing, nothing in return.

Picture the old man opening an envelope. Picture him recognizing the shapes of the writing, the twists and turns. Picture him looking at the lines and curves of the words. He could not make sense of the shapes. He could not turn lines and curves into meaning.

People who loved the old man may have thought he died. They may have thought, no news from America is not good news. Our Georg surely would have written by now. Something unimaginably awful must have befallen him.

The old man never let anyone know he couldn't read. He was too proud. I knew this about him. I could tell. I can always tell. It's one of my skills.

They almost didn't let him into Ellis Island because of his nose. The air-writing. Retardation, they thought, because of his nose going around and around and the look on his face because of his concentration. They almost chalked his coat with a white X, which meant they were going to send him back. It was only at the last minute that the old man realized why they were looking at him that way and he stopped tracing the flag in front of the Ellis Island building with his nose. He stood perfectly still and put a very intelligent look on his face. This is how I picture him, in his olden-days coat with the round collar and a dark hat, and boots that laced up high and were wearing through at the bottom, and one small satchel. That's what they called duffels back then: *satchels.* He stood straight. He looked intelligent. He willed them with all his might to let him in.

*I've come this far,* he willed them. *Let me in.*

The old man didn't speak English yet. He would have willed them in his own, lost language, without seeing the image of the words in his mind. Everything in his body would have been bent into the willing. *Let me in, let me in, let me in.*

The old man's little brother had known how to read. I know this because the old man told me.

"Eli was very good in school," he said to me once during the oral history.

Eli knew that his brother could not read, so Eli would do the reading for the both of them while Georg, the old man, would go out and get a job and support them both. That was the plan. The old man never told me that but still, I know. I believe it to be true.

But the old man came alone to America.

You could write a book report about the old man. You could use his real name and the true facts of his life. His life could be a historical biography, like Eli Whitney or Julia Ward Howe. His life could be boiled down to a two-page plot synopsis. You could include his boyhood in a country that doesn't exist anymore, his coming to America at age seventeen, his job as a metalworker, and how he ended up at Nine Mile Trailer Park in Sterns, New York. You could call the book report *Georg Kominsky: American Immigrant.*

That's a book report I would not write.

I decided to make a show of nonreading solidarity with the old man.

I cut the labels off all the cans in the can cupboard. When I was done, I had three dozen labelless cans. The big fat ones were plum tomato cans. They stood out. But all the others, the other thirty-one cans, were anonymous. No pictures, no words. No identifying characteristics.

The cans lined up nicely, stacked one on top of the other, nothing to tell them apart. I was in the dark. Helpless. Nothing I could do would reveal the meaning of these cans other than opening them up.

Tamar was not pleased.

"What the hell's going on here, Miss?" she said when she opened up the can cupboard. Tamar prefers to eat out of cans and jars. She likes food that comes in glass and tin packages. Sometimes she heats them up, sometimes she doesn't.

All the nameless cans shone in the overhead light. They were pretty, shining like that. Tamar crossed her arms and leaned against the counter. She had a look in her eyes.

"For school," I said. "They're doing a label drive."

She just looked at me.

"We each have to bring in three dozen labels."

She kept on looking.

"For reading," I said. "It's a literacy drive. Literacy is very important."

Still looking. She didn't budge. That's one of her skills.

"What's going on here, Clara?"

There was nothing I could say that would be true without giving away the old man's secret.

"I got going and I couldn't stop," I said.

Still she kept looking at me.

"Is there something you're not telling me?" she said.

"I got going and I couldn't stop," I said again. I kept seeing the words in my head: *I got going and I couldn't stop, I got going and I couldn't stop, I got going and I couldn't—*

"Stop," I said.

Tamar was taking all the cans out of the cupboard. She put them in a brown paper Jewell's Grocery bag and handed them over to me.

"They're yours, Clara," she said. "You can have a mystery food dinner party. I expect replacement cans to be in the can cupboard by Thursday evening."

No plan. No instructions. That's Tamar. She's a you made your bed, you lie in it kind of person. I watched her fix herself a bowl of Cheerios with a banana and raisins and sugar in it and eat it up. That was her dinner. It looked pretty good.

• • •

I took the Jewell's bag of unidentifiable cans down to the old man's the next night, which was Wednesday, choir practice night. Tamar didn't say anything when she dropped me off and saw me haul it out of the back seat. Three dozen cans is a lot. Heavy. Awkward. The bag split halfway down to the old man's house. The lady who lives two trailers down from the old man and wears men's winter boots pushed her living room curtain aside and watched me pick them up.

Did she come out to help? No.

I put a few cans in my jacket pocket and carried as many as I could in my arms and hands. Then I put them all down and put just one large can on top of my head. That's the way African women carry water, in jugs on top of their head. If they can do it, I can too. I tried walking that way. It's quite difficult. You can't look down with your whole head. You have to trust where you're going. Little steps.

The old man opened the door for me. He reached out and plucked the one can from my head. Then he handed me another Jewell's bag, plastic this time. He took another one and we went back to the cans lying in the snow. They shone in the light from the one Nine Mile Trailer Park streetlamp. I pretended the streetlamp was the moon, shining down on the cans.

"I brought dinner," I said. "It's a mystery dinner. We will have no idea what we're eating until we open up the cans."

One of the things about the old man was that he didn't question.

"All right," he said.

In the trailer I was going to make the old man close his eyes. I was going to wrap a dish towel around his head for a blindfold, then I realized it wouldn't matter. What was there to read? What was there to give away the secret? Everything was unknown. That was the whole point of the show of solidarity.

"Pick a can," I said. "Any can."

He picked one, then I picked one. Then he picked another one.

"Three," I said. "That should be good enough. With three we should get in at least two of the four basic food groups."

The old man got out his can opener.

"Can #1?" I said.

"Creamed corn," he said. "Can #1 is creamed corn."

"Can #2?"

"Corned beef hash, from the looks of it."

"#3?"

"Sauerkraut."

We heated up the food and ate it. The old man used a soup spoon to eat everything. No fork. The old man didn't like to waste utensils. Why use two when one will do? In solidarity, I used only a soup spoon, too. Things taste different when you don't use a fork.

"Not bad," I said.

The old man didn't say anything. He didn't usually say anything when he was eating. What he did was look down at his plate and eat steadily and quietly until all the food was gone. Then he picked up his plate and carried it over to his miniature sink and ran water on it.

My heart was not in the dinner. It didn't feel like a show of solidarity to me. Creamed corn, sauerkraut, and corned beef hash. It wasn't so bad. It was a regular dinner, just that we didn't know what we would be eating before we ate it. Nothing lost, nothing gained. No pain involved. What was the point?

• • •

It didn't use to be a shameful thing, not knowing how to read. In many countries of the world almost no one knew how to read. Take China. Only the rulers had enough time to learn how to read and write. That's what a book I read said. *Keep the workers down!* Make a written language so hard to learn that someone with no spare time would never be able to. Never write. Never read. Spend your life cutting stone for the rulers who lay around reading and writing their nearly impossible language.

That's what the book said.

It's an actual book. I didn't make it up.

Think of what the old man lost, not reading: jobs, because he couldn't read the want ads. Doctor appointments, because he couldn't read the reminder slip. Electricity and phone and gas and heat, turned off because he didn't read the bills. Packages sent to him, because he couldn't understand the post office pickup notice. Friends, because he didn't write back. Family, because they never heard from him again.

I thought of the old man as a young man, a boy of eleven, struggling across torrential floodwaters to save a baby wrapped in a yellow blanket, crying in the crook of a black locust tree.

"Clara?"

The old man was standing by the sink in his trailer. He held a dishcloth in his hand. He had rinsed and dried the nameless solidarity cans.

"Clara? Did you hear it?"

"Yes," I said. "Yes, I did hear it."

The old man gave me a look.

"And what did you hear?" he said.

"The baby."

"What baby?"

"The baby you saved in the flood," I said. "The baby in the yellow blanket."

The old man folded his dishcloth. He had a precise way of folding his dishcloth, and a precise way of hanging it on his oven door.

"I saved a baby in a yellow blanket?" he said.

"Yes."

I could hear that baby crying still, laid in the crotch of the black locust tree. What had happened to her mother? How could a baby come to be laid in a tree during the worst flood in the village's history? In my mind the young Georg struggled and fought his way across the raging current, bent on saving the helpless child.

"I was talking about the owl by Nine Mile Creek," he said. "You can hear it sometimes on a night like tonight."

I looked at him. It was hard to come back from the flood, hard to unimagine him as a boy.

"And this baby, what about this baby in the yellow blanket?" he said.

"Nothing," I said.

A single thought spun out of air turns into a baby in a yellow blanket, longing for its mother. But there was no baby in a yellow blanket. The old man never struggled through foaming water and tumbling debris to rescue a crying infant perched in the crotch of a black locust tree. That was my story, not the old man's story. None of it happened, none of it was real. Still, it's what I believed to be true.

Again he asked me:

"What happened to the baby in the yellow blanket?"

I wanted to say, *You tell me. You were the one who saved that baby's life.*

"That baby never existed," I said. "End of story."

The old man turned his hands palms up. That's something he used to do. He would turn them up and study each palm, tracing the lines. After a while of the old man studying his hands and waiting for me to talk, and me not talking, he went to his bedroom and brought me back a brown paper bag. Inside was a lantern, a regular-size pioneer lantern made of tin.

"To replace your missing earring," he said.

"This is not the sort of lantern I intended," I said. "You said you'd make me a lantern *earring*. This is a real lantern."

He had made it out of my leftover plum tomato cans, the ones I had strung in his weeping willow. You could still see the red tomato labeling on the inside of the lantern. He had punched holes into it in decorative patterns, like the kind of decorative patterns the pioneers used to make. I had seen these patterns in old library books. The old man had cut thin strips of aluminum from the cans and curled them into little curlicues and attached them to the top and bottom of the lantern for decoration. He had put a nail into the bottom of the lantern and spiked a candle on the nail. He had made a carrying handle for the lantern out of twisted wire.

"This is not an earring," I said.

"Lanterns should be useful as well as beautiful," the old man said.

I thought of my missing lantern earring, sinking ever deeper into the snow and mud. I imagined floodwaters sweeping it away, helpless in the torrent, down the Nine Mile Creek and into the Utica floodplain. Swamp gas enveloping my lovely earring in its evil vapors. Swamp worms curving around it, thinking it was some kind of treasure.

The old man took one of his furnace matches, gigantic long ones, and lit the candle. It was getting dark outside. Across Nine Mile Creek I could see the stained-glass windows of the church where Tamar and the other choir people were practicing. The old man put the lantern on the kitchen table and turned out all the lights. We sat there at his table looking at the lantern. He had punched winter into the lantern: snowflakes, stars, a snowman.

"I hate winter," I said. "I hate snow. Winter is what killed Baby Girl."

The old man turned the lantern around. On the other side he'd punched in summer: a sun with big rays, a flower, a robin. Across Nine Mile Creek the stained-glass windows went dark. Tamar would be driving up to the trailer park in exactly six minutes. She's never late.

"This is a pioneer lantern," the old man said. "For doing winter chores."

"But what I wanted was a new lantern earring for my one remaining lantern."

"It never would have been an exact match," he said. "It never would have been the original."

He turned the lantern around. Winter shone out at me. He turned it again, and it was summer. Outside the trailer it was pitch black. Tamar would be driving up in exactly three minutes. She would honk the horn and reach across to open up the door for me. It doesn't open from the outside anymore. The old man turned the lantern around and kept on turning it. The candle stayed steady. It was stuck firmly on its spike. Stars turned into sun, snowflakes into flowers, a snowman was a robin with a big fat worm. I stared at the turning lantern. I held my head straight and did not blink, trying hard to train my eyes to see the possibility of beauty.

# Chapter Six

Tamar has a father, which means that I have a grandfather. If A is Tamar, and B is her father, and C is me, the relationship is mathematically clear. He was in the truck when I was born in the blizzard.

"He lives way up in the Adirondacks," Tamar said years ago, when I first asked her about him and she forbade me to mention him ever again. "Near the Vermont border. And that's all you need to know."

Way up in the Adirondacks near the Vermont border sounds like hermit territory to me. Is my grandfather a hermit? Why not? Nary a single visit to his only living granddaughter makes my grandfather a hermit in my book.

My grandfather lives in a tent in the middle of a primeval forest in the Adirondacks. You may think that upstate New York has no primeval forests left. You may think that there are no primeval forests on the east coast of America, nor in the middle west, nor on the west coast with the exception of the ones in Oregon and Washington that everyone knows about.

You would be wrong.

There is a small primeval forest in the hermit country of upstate New York, just before the Vermont border. It is composed of old-growth trees, trees that are more than five hundred years old. These trees have existed since before the American Revolutionary War. They were here when Columbus sailed onto Plymouth Rock, if he actually did. They were here for the Civil War. The Green Mountain Boys snuck through this primeval forest on their way to fight the graycoats.

Am I telling the truth?

I very well may be.

Who would know?

Is there anyone who has inspected every square inch of the Adirondack Park? Have helicopters and airplanes and surveyors and bloodhounds straining at the leash and hikers and campers and forest rangers mapped out every square inch of the Empire State? Has every square inch been traversed and retraversed? Is there anyone alive who can say with absolute certainty: *"No. Not one square inch of Adirondack woods consists of primeval forest."*

Do you see what I mean?

The truth can be sought. The truth can be hunted down. The truth can be your one and only rule, but it is slippery. It hides. You think you've got it pinned down, but you don't.

When I first started imagining my grandfather up in the Adirondacks, I wondered what he lived on. Was he totally self-sufficient? Did he trap furs in the winter and barter them for essential supplies? Every hermit must have some essential supplies, such as matches, flour, cooking oil. A hammer, a hunting rifle, and ammunition. Candles. Cornmeal. Tobacco, for the pipe he smoked while hunched over his campfire in the dead of winter. My hermit grandfather knew the fearsome power of snow and cold.

I still think about my hermit grandfather. I still wonder about him.

Some would say that I made him up, that he never existed. But I can see him in my mind, walking silently through the woods on the breast of new-fallen snow. Doesn't that make him real in a way?

"Ma, is your father a hermit?"

I asked Tamar that, even though she had forbidden me ever to mention her father. Tamar looked at me.

"A hermit? My father, a hermit?"

"Yes. That is the question," I said.

"What possesses you, Clara? What goes through your brain?"

I said nothing. In the face of Tamar's derision my dream was already crumbling into dust and blowing away like sand in a Thebes desert storm. I wanted to hang on to my hermit. Already I loved him.

In certain snow conditions you can't see your hand in front of your face. Tamar and I were coming home from Boonville one winter day when I was nine. She was driving. It was whiteout conditions: snow blowing fast and furious, horizontal because of the wind. When you look out a window and you see snow blowing horizontally, it's instinct to turn your head sideways.

Horizontal snow is a world gone awry.

Tamar and I were a couple miles out of Boonville, heading south to North Sterns, when it turned from slanted to horizontal and intermittently to blizzard. It was only midafternoon. Everything was a fury of white.

"Do not dissolve, Clara," she said.

Tamar knows how I hate the snow.

She opened her window and stuck her head out. She slowed the car down but she didn't stop. It's better not to stop unless there's a parking lot or something. On a back road you have no idea where you're stopping. A plow, a sander—anything—can come up behind you on a back road in a blizzard and smash you to bits. That's the risk you run, stopping.

Tamar had her head stuck out the window. Snow was already clumping on her hair and her eyelashes. Her head was tilted and she squinted against the snow. I saw what she was doing. She was sighting her way by the telephone poles. She was going just fast enough to find the next one after the first one receded. From telephone pole to telephone pole, Tamar kept the car going.

"Hang tough, Clara," she yelled with her head out the window.

I hooked up my personal backup bungee cord belt system. I use it only in dire straits. Two bungee cords, one orange and one black. Emergency colors. One stretches from Tamar's headrest over my left shoulder and fastens onto the door handle. The other stretches from my headrest and fastens onto the stick shift. They cross in my middle and pinion me.

Tamar's head was out the window. She didn't see me hooking up the bungee cords. They're for extreme conditions only. Tamar hates them.

"Worse than useless," she said when I first devised the system. "Those bungees'll kill you before they'll save you from anything."

She unhooked the orange one and shook it in my face.

"You see this hook? Any kind of crash, even a fender bender, this thing'd come unhooked and slash your face up. Or gouge your eye out."

She let go of the hook and I hooked it up again. She could tell I was not going to be intimidated.

"You are an odd child, Clara Winter," she said. "You are truly strange."

But ever since that day south of Boonville, when she was sighting her way by the telephone poles, she hasn't said a word. She lets me hook up the bungees. They're only for when I feel extreme danger.

Sometimes Tamar's unarguability is useful. When we were driving in that blizzard and she was sighting her way along the road by the telephone poles, it was useful. I was bungeed in and chanting. If you chant when you're in grave danger, you can transport yourself into a world of safety. You just chant and chant and chant, the same thing over and over, until you feel yourself transported.

*mm, mm, mm.*

That's my chant. I don't want it to be anything that makes sense, because then I would focus on the sense I was making instead of the world of safety. It's all related to the ability to read. Are you beginning to see that? If you say something that makes sense, and you're a reader, the words scroll across the bottom of your mind and there you are. You're stuck. You're focusing on the meaning of the words, the shape of the letters, rather than the meaningless sound of the chant itself and the world of safety it's taking you into.

"Hold it together, Clara," Tamar yelled in from the window. She had one hand on the steering wheel and one hand on the open window. I chanted and chanted but I was not transported. The bungee cords held me against the back of the seat and I opened my eyes to watch Tamar's hand curled tight around the steering wheel like a spider on a web.

Then we went into the ditch.

Immediately Tamar's head was back inside the car. She rolled up her window and shook her head so that the caked snow flew all over the dashboard. The snow on her eyelashes started to melt and melted snow ran down her cheeks. She reached across with her frozen hands and hooked her fingers through my bungee cords.

"You will, not, fall, apart, Clara Winter," she said. "Hear me?"

I could feel how cold her hand was even through my jacket, sweater, turtleneck, and T-shirt.

"We are in the ditch," she said. "Being in the ditch is not the end of the world."

She forgets. It *was* the end of the world for Baby Girl.

Tamar started to undo the bungees. Her fingers were so cold that they didn't bend right. When she got them undone, she undid the seatbelt.

"We're walking," she said. "Bundle up."

She was unarguable. I had to crawl over the hump and then over her seat to get out, because the car was tilted into the ditch. She was already marching ahead. The car was already being snowed over. It was a true blizzard.

Did she think about my sister?

Did she blame herself? My grandfather? The snow?

On she marched. I ran to keep up.

"Wait," I screamed. The wind took my words and whipped them away. I kept screaming out the word: *wait, wait*, but

Tamar's back kept getting away from me. I looked to my left. A telephone pole. You could barely see it through the driving snow. I looked for the next one. I couldn't see it. Then she was there, Tamar, standing in front of me.

"Keep, up," she yelled. "Do, you, hear, me? Keep, up. I do not plan to lose my daughter in a blizzard."

She puts it out of her mind. *You already did lose your daughter in a blizzard.* I couldn't say that to Tamar though. After I showed her Baby Girl Winter's death certificate, Tamar told me the bare minimum: the truck, the blizzard, the ditch. To her it was as if my baby sister never drew breath. Which is another of my questions: did my baby sister draw breath? Did her miniature lungs fill even once with frozen Adirondack air?

I saw that Tamar was wearing her loafers. She didn't even have her boots on.

"Ma? You don't have your boots on," I yelled.

I had to yell. That was the only way you could make yourself heard that day. She didn't say anything. She just kept marching. Her loafers were filled with snow. Packed with it. I did not allow myself to think of how cold her feet must be. In the pioneer days it was common to lose toes to frostbite. Pioneers were always getting lost in the snow. In the pioneer days blizzards were worse than they are now. Pioneers would often go out to the barn to milk their cow and then get lost on the way back to the cabin. The wind and snow drove so hard back in those days that they would walk right on past the cabin, just missing the log corner. They would walk right on into the wilderness. Lost pioneers would not be found until spring, when the snow melted. There they would be, curled up in a fetal position.

They say that death by freezing is not such a bad way to go.

Once you get cold enough you actually feel warm. This is what I have read.

I wonder what their last thoughts were, though. I wonder what they thought when they knew they'd walked long enough to get back to the cabin. Did they try to turn around? Which way was the way back? Which way was north? This was in the days before compasses, probably. In those days they had only the stars to navigate by. With the snow swirling all around them, and the darkness of the sky above, nothing to light their way, the candle in their tin lantern blown out by the howling wind, I just wonder what those pioneers thought.

When Tamar was giving birth in the truck tipped over in the ditch, did she know that one of her babies was going to die? Could she possibly have foreseen what was going to happen? Did she even know she was going to have twins?

"Ma! Did you know you were going to have twins?"

I yelled this to her back. Her loafers disappeared into the mounds of snow with every step. My boots had my snowpants pulled over them. My feet were protected against the blowing snow.

She didn't answer. She never does. She won't talk about it. She leaves me to wonder about it myself, to try to guess what happened. She keeps me in the dark.

It took us a couple of hours of blizzard walking to reach a house. After a while I put my head down and focused on Tamar's loafers. They were dark brown when she lifted them, with packed white around her feet. I kept my eyes focused on her feet. They became a visual blizzard chant: *don't let Tamar's feet freeze.* A rhythm set itself up in my head: *don't* let Ta*mar's* feet *freeze.* One step for every emphasis. *Don't let Tamar's feet freeze.* The snow piled up on my neck. It sifted underneath my scarf, melted against my neck, and ran down my back. Then the process started all over again. Pile, sift, melt, run. Everything took on a rhythm in that blizzard. We walked and we walked. Walking became the only thing I could remember. I turned myself into the walking. There was nothing to think about because I was no longer a person. I was no longer a sentient being. I was no longer even a reader. My thoughts did not scroll across the bottom of my mind because I had no thoughts.

That's the one time in my life that I was not a human being. I was only a thing that walked.

Tamar's loafers that were dark brown and packed white around her socks changed direction. They turned. Because I was no longer a thinking being I did not know if they turned right or left. I followed because that was what the thing I had become did; it followed Tamar's loafers.

Tamar's loafers stopped. There was a tinkling sound outside the deafness of falling snow. Tamar's loafers were lifting up high in the whiteness and then disappearing. I stood there because they were gone. There was nothing left to follow.

Then she grabbed me. The second she touched me I went back to being a human being. Sentience returned. Words again started subtitling my brain: *don't let Tamar's feet freeze.*

"In," she shouted. "Get your butt inside. Climb right through that window. Now."

Then we were inside. It was somebody's house. Somebody who was not there. Where were they? South for the winter? Immediately the person who was not there became a Florida person to me. I could see her, lying on the sand in the sun with a small, thick paperback book facedown next to her. There was a thermostat on the wall and I saw Tamar go over to it. She angled her elbow toward it and gave it a jab, and then there was a sound of *heat*. Nothing is like the sound of a furnace leaping into action, lunging and thrumming somewhere way down in the basement, when you twirl a thermostat in the winter.

"Why'd you use your elbow?" I said.

My words sounded unusual. They came out thick, like slush, into the frozen air.

Tamar didn't answer. She was already gone. I heard water running. She was in the kitchen running water. Why weren't the pipes frozen? In an Adirondack winter, pipes are always frozen. I went into the kitchen of the Florida person's house.

"Why aren't the pipes frozen?" I said. Still slushy-sounding.

"Why *would* the pipes be frozen? Whoever owns this house is probably stuck in the blizzard, just like us."

My Florida person faded away. She turned into an Adirondacks lady sitting in Tam's Diner on Route 12, cupping her cold fingers around a mug of hot coffee, her car in the parking lot disappearing minute by minute under the snow.

"Oh," I said. "Why'd you use your elbow to turn on the heat?"

"Because my fingers are too cold to move," Tamar said.

She was sitting on a chair with her feet in the sink. She was running water on her feet that still had their loafers and socks on. It was hot water. I could see the steam.

*Don't let Tamar's feet freeze.*

I went over to the sink. I took my hands out from my armpits where I had been keeping them warm. Always put frozen hands in your armpits. That's something I learned from the pioneer books. I pulled at Tamar's loafers until they fell off. They clunked into the sink. They weighed a thousand pounds each. I pulled her white socks off. They weighed a hundred pounds each.

Her feet were white.

Not a good sign.

Dead white is a sign of frozen flesh. What is hoped for, when removing a pioneer's shoes and socks, is pink skin. Roaring red skin is even better. White is not what you want.

"Shut up, Clara," Tamar said before I even said a word. "I don't want to hear it. Keep your pioneers to yourself."

The hot water ran and ran. My cold feet in my moon boots were getting warm. My fingers were warm. The furnace thrummed and hummed. The person's house was getting warm.

"Go cover that broken window with a coat or something, would you Clara, please."

That was unlike Tamar. Please is a word not prevalent in Tamar's lexicon. I went and covered the window. Tamar ran warm water over her feet for a long time. I stood beside her and watched her feet. After a while she bent over and held her hands under the faucet too. Then she picked up the drainplug and plugged the drain.

"Dumb," she said. "Running all this hot water. Probably used up most of it."

Dumb is not a word used by Tamar. The hot water filled the kitchen sink and Tamar turned it off. Her fingers were bright red. That's a good sign. She submerged her feet in the sink.

"Dumb," she said again.

Tamar was crying. Tamar was crying and calling herself dumb.

"Ma?"

She shook her bright red hand at me. Drops of warm water spattered on my face. She turned her head away from me so that her brown hair hung down and I couldn't see her.

"Sorry, Clara."

Nor does Tamar say she's sorry.

"It's all right," I said.

It wasn't though. It was not all right. It has never been all right.

Winter is out there. It waits. It bides its time. Sometimes, when you're lulled into a false sense of security, it comes roaring out at you and tries to destroy you. It is ruthless. It has no mercy. Victims fall prey to it. The bodies of dead pioneers, found only after the spring thaw, are buried beneath the ground. Baby Girl died because of winter.

Tamar's shoulders shook with her crying.

"Did you try to save her?" I said.

That's a question that demands an answer.

But no answer was forthcoming.

We stayed in the kitchen for a long time. The furnace kept humming. There was no moment when the furnace heated the house as hot as we wanted it and then shut off because there was no more heating to do. That point was never reached. The furnace kept on going, and we kept on staying. We stayed in that person's house for three days, until the plow went through. It came through in darkest night. We were sleeping in the person's bed. I kept dreaming of her as a Florida person, lying on her Florida beach, drinking soda from a glass with a small pink umbrella on it. The house was eighty-eight degrees. That's the warmest Tamar has ever had a house. Usually she sets the thermostat at sixty-three.

"Put on a sweater," she says when I start to shiver.

That's one of her flat Tamar statements. But in that person's house she cranked the heat up as high as it could go.

"We'll fix the window," she said. "We'll pay their oil bill. They won't mind."

Tamar's feet hurt when they thawed.

"Damn it," she said, when they had been in the water a long time. "Damn it."

She gritted her teeth. I could hear them gritting.

"Is the feeling coming back?" I said.

That's a good sign. What you want is for your feet to hurt horribly, to be hideously painful. That means that the blood is returning to your extremities. Your feet will be saved. You won't have to chop them off. Gangrene will not set in and it's very possible that no toes will be lost.

She didn't answer. It's rare that Tamar feels the need to answer every question I ask her, despite the fact that most of the questions I ask her are ones that demand answers.

"Are they hurting?" I asked.

"They are hurting like hell," she said.

"Good. That's a good sign."

After a long time Tamar let the water drain out of the sink and she dried her feet. Her hands were still bright red and her fingers did not move swiftly. Her feet were also bright red except for a few small white patches on some of the toes.

"You see those small white patches?" I said. "They may very well be frostbite."

"Enough, Clara."

I did not mention frostbite again. But still, I could tell. I've read enough pioneer books to know that small white patches mean frostbite. When we got home Tamar went to the doctor at Slocum-Dickson in Utica, who confirmed my diagnosis. Her feet hurt her now when it gets cold. Her toes are especially painful. I can tell. She walks in a certain way. Tamar would never admit to it but still, I know. Once frozen, your flesh will never be completely unfrozen. The memory of cold becomes a part of you. You never forget.

My hermit grandfather would have known better than to venture out in the winter. My grandfather knew full well the power of a winter storm. He had watched it wreak devastation on his own family, for it was he who was behind the wheel of the truck when it went skidding into the ditch. Sometimes I strain my memory, trying to remember my grandfather's face. I must have seen it when I was born, even if only for a moment. I looked at Tamar, kneading her thawed feet, and it occurred to me that she might look like her father. She might be his spitting image. How would I know?

"Ma, do you think that a newborn is capable of remembering a face?" I said to Tamar.

"No."

"Not at all?"

"Not at all. A newborn doesn't even know what a face is. A newborn has never been outside the uterus; a newborn wouldn't know the difference between a human being and a goldfish."

Coming from Tamar, that was the answer I expected. Everything Tamar says must be taken with a grain of salt. You have to filter everything through the knowledge of what you know about Tamar.

"Do you believe in baby purgatory?" I asked Tamar.

"Enough, Clara."

"But do you?"

"I said, enough."

She wiggled her toes up and down. Her toes moved slowly, as if they had forgotten how to wiggle. I watched her right eye and saw it squint nearly shut while the left stayed wide open. Did my grandfather's eyes do that, too?

You can't blame my grandfather for becoming a hermit. He shunned society in favor of solitude. He had only his own thoughts for company. He depended on himself and only himself, except for his twice-yearly visits to town to trade his furs for cash to buy necessities. Maybe my hermit grandfather sang songs to himself at night, when he lay on his pallet. Maybe he went walking in the moonlight, only the stars and the silent moon and the watchful nocturnal animals as witness.

Maybe he thought about Tamar. He might have thought about her, his only daughter, and wondered what she was doing. He may have thought about me, the grandchild he had not seen since the day she was born. He might have thought about the other granddaughter, the ghost baby, the one he could not save.

Did he try?

Did he attempt everything he possibly could to try to save my baby sister's life?

"Tamar, did my grandfather have any paramedic training?"

"Why do you ask, Clara?"

"Just wondering."

"The answer is no. To my knowledge my father had no paramedical training."

"So he would not have been able to resuscitate a hypothet-ical dead newborn?"

"Enough, Clara," Tamar said. She held her hurting feet with both hands, twisting them to the right and back to the left. "Enough, enough, enough."

# Chapter Seven

The old man was a hero for many reasons, not the least of which was that he once escaped from the solitary confinement to which he had been unfairly sentenced. Most often a solitary confinement is a hole in the ground, covered with a wooden door. Such was the case with the old man. When a prisoner is bad enough or, like the old man, unfairly sentenced for a fake offense—backtalk to a guard—they chain his legs and arms and drag him to a hole in the ground. They remove the chains and throw him in. They lock the wooden door in place and that's it. Once, possibly twice a day, the door is opened and a bucket of water and another bucket of slop are lowered into the hole. That's what the old man lived on. There was nowhere to go to the bathroom in the old man's solitary confinement except in the mud at the bottom of the hole.

I can picture the old man as a young man, crouched in the bottom of the muddy pit, curling himself into a fetal position on the filthy scrap of old horse blanket that the guards had thrown down on him. I can see that poor young man so clearly, reciting stories and poems from his childhood in an effort to keep from going insane.

If you can see it so clearly in your mind, it's real. Isn't it?

Few prisoners survive more than a few weeks in solitary confinement. If they are not allowed into the light of day within a fairly short time, they start to rot. Once you start to rot death comes quickly. People need light. They need sunshine in order to keep on living. They need sound, which is another thing that does not exist in solitary confinement.

How did the old man survive? He had a secret life. He knew from the very first day in the hole of solitary confinement that he would not be able to survive unless he had two things: a dream and an escape route. The very first night, he broke off a tree root that was growing into the side of the hole. For the next year, he used that root to dig silently at night. Using mental maps, he tunneled his way directly underneath the prison kitchen. Eventually, by tracking the vibrations of the ground above his head, he figured out where the prison kitchen root cellar was and tunneled up to it.

This took a total of eleven months. He kept track of the passing days in his head. Each night he made up legends and myths and stories. Georg Kominsky knew that unless he exercised his brain as well as his body, both would atrophy. What kept Georg going? What prevented him from giving in to despair?

His dream.

He dreamed of his metalworking tools.

Georg Kominsky had a vision and he did not allow himself to swerve from that vision. Despite the cockroaches that swarmed over his pallet at night and the pale worms that writhed in his nightly food bucket, he forced himself to eat and sleep and exercise and make up legends. He did not once allow the thought of death to enter his mind. Night after night, day after day, the old man kept on going.

It might seem that a dream of metalworking alone would not be enough. It might seem that someone would need more than the thought of tin snips, a solder iron, and a forge to stay alive.

Not if you were the old man. I know this because that's what he told me. Once, a few weeks after I told him about Baby Girl Winter and how I hated being without her, the old man looked at me and said, "You only need one thing, Clara."

"One what?"

"One thing to keep you going. One thing will do."

I looked at him. We were outside at his forge. He was working on a lantern, soldering decorative strips to the sides.

"Well, what's your one thing then?" I said.

He pulled his safety glasses over his eyes and touched the tip of the solder iron to the tin. Gray metal-melt trickled down the side.

"This. Making useful and beautiful objects of metal. This, and the memory of my mother in a dark room, singing to my younger brother."

"That's it?" I said.

"That's it."

"That's not one thing, that's two."

"Then I'm a lucky man," he said.

There came a night when the old man broke through into the root cellar. From then on he led a secret life. Solitary confinement by day, prison kitchen by night. In the early hours of each morning, this brave man made his way into the prison kitchen. Careful never to take more than would be noticed, he built up his strength with raw turnips, raw potatoes, and left-over bread. He used the prison sink to bathe in. He shaved with a kitchen knife and the light of the moon. He did calisthenics to keep his muscles strong. Every night he stretched and stretched to stay limber.

When he had completed his nightly foray, the old man covered his tunnel opening with a wooden crate full of potatoes and headed back to the hole.

He never gave up.

He did not allow himself to think beyond the moment. He did not allow himself to think of the day beyond the present day, the weeks stretching into months, into years, into a lifetime.

He never once thought: my youth has passed me by and I will die in this hole, an old, old man.

He thought instead of his tin snips, his forge, his solder iron, and his mother in a dark room, singing.

After ten years they opened the wooden cover to the hole and brought him up into the light of day. Blinking and squinting at the sunlight that he had not seen more than a glimpse of for a decade, Georg Kominsky regained his freedom. He lives on in the hearts and minds of his fellow prisoners, a symbol of the human spirit determined to survive at all odds.

"What would you like to do tonight?" the old man said one Wednesday night when I arrived. I looked out the window above the old man's sink. The choir members hadn't even turned the lights on in the Twin Churches. We had two hours.

"I would like to have some hot chocolate," I said.

I got out one of my hot chocolate packets from the cupboard. In the beginning, the old man bought me hot chocolate packets from Jewell's. But when I figured out that he was poor I insisted on bringing my own. I used to get hot chocolate packets free at the bank, at the little refreshment table in the corner where the armchairs are. There's a coffeemaker and a small wicker basket of tea bags, coffee bags, and hot chocolate packets. There are wooden stirrers and fake cream, which must be spelled creme or kreme. You cannot use the word *cream* if it's not real cream. That's the law.

They frown on nongrownups who avail themselves of the little refreshment table, but I used to take the packets anyway.

"It's for a good cause," I said once to the bank lady when I saw her giving me the once-over.

The old man was a good cause.

I don't go in the bank anymore.

I put hot water on the miniature stove and waited for it to boil. It's a fallacy that a watched pot never boils. I've proved it wrong many a time. While I was watching the pot and thinking about the young Georg Kominsky tunneling for ten years through dirt, the old man washed the supper dishes. The old man could stand in one place and reach the sink, the stove, the refrigerator, and the dish cupboard. He had just enough dishes. Two mugs. Three plates. Three bowls. Three forks. Three spoons. One table knife and one little sharp knife. He didn't need any more knives because the old man rarely ate anything that required cutting. You might think that having three plates and bowls is having one too many, but you would be wrong. What about the serving plate and the serving bowl? You've got to have an extra to serve from.

The old man had white plates with orange borders. Sad to say, orange is my least favorite color. The only way I like orange is as it occurs in nature, for example, orange poppies in gardens, orange tiger lilies by the side of the road, orange and black Monarch butterflies, orange Indian paintbrush in the field. When orange occurs elsewhere, as in borders on white plates, it is abhorrent. It is a crime against nature. That is my belief.

"Where did you get your white plates with the orange borders?" I asked the old man as he was drying them. He used to dry every dish separately. Forks, spoons, everything. He was fastidious about his dish drying.

"Scavenging night," he said.

The old man was a wonderful scavenger. I sometimes accompanied him on scavenging expeditions. He had a sixth sense.

"You've got to have the eye," he said.

I don't have the eye yet, but I'm trying. I'm training my eyes to be like the old man. It's difficult for two reasons: (a) I know how to read and he didn't, and (b) he saw possibility everywhere.

When you know how to read you can never get away from it. Your eye goes to words first and everything else second. The old man was not hampered by the knowledge of letters. His eye could roam free. He could take in the big picture, whereas I am bound to words first and foremost. Now that I know this I sometimes try to remember being a baby, before I was trapped by words. What was it like? I ask myself. I narrow my eyes and try not to see words and printing and letters. It's hopeless. I'm a reader.

While he dried the dishes I asked him my death row question again.

"I will ask you a variation of the question you never answered," I said. "Electric chair or life in solitary confinement with worms in your meal bucket every night and only a scrap of horse blanket to sleep on: which would you choose?"

He hung his dish towel over the oven door handle to dry. He always hung it in exactly the same way.

"Are they my only choices?"

"They are your only choices."

"I ask because there are many other ways to live and die."

"There are more ways to live and die, Horatio, than are dreamt of in your universe," I said. "But you are allowed only two. Which do you choose?"

"Which would *you* choose?"

He used to do that sometimes, turn the tables.

"I believe, sir, that you were the one asked the question," I said.

The old man finished washing and drying his dishes. No answer was forthcoming.

"It's scavenging night tonight," he said. "Do you want to go looking with me?"

"Sure," I said.

"Do you need anything special?"

Yes, I thought. I need a sister. I need my Baby Girl.

"How about cookie cutters?" I said. "Small metal objects that are useful as well as beautiful."

Tamar has a small cheesecloth bag of cookie cutters in our junk drawer at home. We don't use them. We don't make cookies. Tamar doesn't believe in sweet things. She has a streak of asceticism in her. She would not admit to it, but she does. If they do it the way it should be done, monks and nuns are ascetics. They live alone in cells. Absolutely bare. Stripped of everything worldly, which means anything colorful, anything frivolous, anything that is not essential to the sustainment of life. If they do it right, monks and nuns go to sleep on hard cots with one blanket in a cell that has one cross hanging on the wall, preferably at the head of their narrow single bed with its one, scratchy, thin, brown, wool blanket, similar to the kind of scrap of horse blanket that the young Georg Kominsky slept with in solitary confinement.

Our small cheesecloth bag of metal cookie cutters contains a bell, a heart, and a star. That's it. You can't get much more basic than that. To my knowledge, they have never been used. The most sugar the antisugar Tamar allows is a teaspoonful on her Cheerios. She's a thin woman, Tamar. Some might call her scrawny.

The old man saw possibility. The old man saw potential in things that I could not. Tinfoil, for instance. A person like the person I used to be would rip off just enough tinfoil to wrap the leftover with, wrap it, and stick it in the refrigerator. But the old man made tinfoil swans out of his leftovers.

"That's a waste of good tinfoil," Tamar said the one time I tried to make something pretty out of two leftover boiled potatoes at home.

I was not doing a good job of it. I tried for a swan first, but that didn't work. Then I tried for a heart shape, but it was lopsided, so I settled for a roll with twisted tinfoil tails.

"It's an abstract sculpture," I said.

"It's an abstract waste," she said.

If I had tried to argue with Tamar about the tinfoil abstract sculpture, I would have said that my abstract sculpture was useful because it protected the boiled potatoes. And that it was beautiful because it was an abstract sculpture. The waste of a few square inches of tinfoil is secondary to the beauty. That's what I would have said, had I tried to argue with Tamar. But the fact is, she's unarguable.

It is not common to find, for example, beautiful cookie cutters set out in the trash. Instead, the old man and I used to find pre—cookie cutters: strips of thin scrap metal behind the service station, for example, or old tin milk crates stacked up behind the Sterns Co-op. The old man had the eye. He could tell what had the potential to become a cookie cutter and what had a different destiny. I could see his eyes going from one trash pile to another. He looked and he kept on looking. Then he would pick something up and put it in the Jewell's bag.

"This has possibility," he said.

Or he said nothing.

There was an abundance of plastic bags that particular night. Thin, filmy plastic bags, the kind you put vegetables in at Jewell's. They were blowing around the trailer park. Patches of white on branches. One puffed up at me like a ghost.

"Why are there so many plastic bags blowing around here?" I asked.

The old man didn't answer. It wasn't a question that demanded an answer anyway. Some questions demand answers; others are rhetorical. I decided to ask a series of rhetorical questions.

"Rhetorical question number one: Why do people choose to let their plastic bags blow around in the wind? Two, would it kill them to put their vegetables all in one brown paper bag instead of a series of plastic bags, one vegetable species in each? Three, do these plastic bag people ever stop to think about the ten thousand years it takes a plastic bag to degrade?"

"Clara," the old man said.

That's all he said. What he meant was: quiet down, please.

I quieted down. We walked up Route 365 into the village of Sterns. Jewell's Grocery was closed, as was Crystal's Diner. The old man spotted a big olive oil can behind Crystal's. There was a picture of Italian hills and an olive tree on the front of the can. It had a big dent. I once remarked on the greenness of the oil I was observing Crystal mix with vinegar.

"That's because it's pure olive oil," Crystal said. "I use it because my grandmother was ¹⁄₁₆ Greek. That's the only part of me that's not Polack, the ¹⁄₆₄ of me that's Greek."

"That's one of Crystal's olive oil cans," I said. "Someone ran over it, looks like."

The old man nodded. He turned it around in his hands, looking at it from all angles. I could tell he was considering. He was mulling over the possibilities in his mind.

"I can see the wheels turning," I said. "Get it?"

"This has possibility," he said.

When he said that, I took the dented olive oil can and studied it myself, for the possibility. I'm training my eye. It's slow going.

The old man: *Dented olive oil can = pre–cookie cutter.*

Me: *Dented olive oil can = ?*

You have to look closely. You have to concentrate. You have to have the ability to see another destiny for something, a fate far removed from its original one. That's what the old man was good at.

"Okay," I said.

I never disagreed with the old man. You're not allowed to argue or disagree when you're an apprentice. You have to have the utmost faith that the master knows full well what he is doing. All things will be revealed to the apprentice in the fullness of time.

The old man held the dented olive oil can in one hand and we walked back to his trailer. The lady two trailers down looked out her window when we passed. She didn't wave. She never waved. Many was the time I considered giving up waving at her, but I kept on. You never know. There may come a time.

The old man washed the can with soap and water and got his tin snips. We sat down at the table and he snipped the can open down each side. He set the dented side apart and laid the others out before us. I watched everything he did. I used to observe every move the old man made when he worked on something. That's how apprentices learn. That's how Paul Revere became the silversmith he was, back in the colonial days. First he was an apprentice, then he was a journeyman, then he was a master.

"Tamar will be here in twenty minutes," I said.

"All right," he said.

The old man tilted his head and studied the pieces of tin. He studied tin, and I studied him. His tin snips lay on the table. That, and his solder iron, were the only two things he brought with him from his country that doesn't exist anymore. They were the only things that stayed with him to the end.

The old man also had a small forge. He kept the forge, along with a vise, in back of his trailer, on the patch of land that ran along Nine Mile Creek. That way the smoke didn't bother anyone. When the old man wanted to do some black-smithing, he used his forge. I used to sit on the bank of Nine Mile Creek and watch the smoke spiral up into the air.

The old man bought the forge and the vise at an auction in North Sterns. Mr. Jewell drove him up there. I know that because I once overheard Mr. Jewell ask the old man how the forge was holding up.

"Good," the old man said.

"The vise too?"

"The vise too."

Later I asked Mr. Jewell how he knew about the forge and the vise.

"Because, Miss Clara Winter, I drove him up to the auction where he bought them," Mr. Jewell said.

After the old man was gone, I found an old Sears Roebuck catalogue at the Back of the Barn Antiques on Route 12 north of Remsen. I went there with Tamar once, so she could visit her friend who works there. Tamar's friend owns a bird who sits on her shoulder all day long. The bird is silent. It is neither a talking nor a singing bird. For a while I thought it was a clip-on bird. That was before it blinked its eye at me and yawned.

In the catalogue there was a picture of a forge and a vise that looked like the old man's forge and vise. Here is the description of the forge from the Sears, Roebuck & Co., Cheapest Supply House on Earth, Chicago, Catalogue No. 111, page 613:

*The Forge. We furnish a lever forge having hearth 18 inches in diameter.*
*It is furnished with 6-inch fan. The gear is the simplest, strongest and best*

*ever put on a forge. Only a slight movement of the lever produces the*
*strongest blast.*

*The Vise. We furnish a wrought iron solid box and screw blacksmith vise,*
*with steel jaws, weighing 35 pounds.*

The vise and the forge came with a complete set of tools, and altogether the complete set cost $25. I asked Mr. Jewell how much the old man had paid for his forge and vise at the auction.

"I wouldn't know, Miss Clara," he said. "Why do you ask?"

The old man had been gone for months by then.

Why did I ask? I wouldn't know.

Next time I went to the old man's, on a Saturday afternoon, the tin-snipped pieces of olive oil can had disappeared from the table. The old man had screwed in large cup hooks all along the top of the far kitchen window frame. Hanging on the hooks were new cookie cutters. If you looked closely, and if you had personal knowledge of their previous life as a dented olive oil can, you might be able to tell that what were now cookie cutters had once been broken pieces of metal.

The olive oil can had been reincarnated as objects of light. One was in the shape of a decorative tin lantern, another was a candelier, another was a candlestick with a cutout of a burning candle in it.

"But soft!" I said. "What light from yonder window breaks? It is the east, and cookie cutters are the sun."

The old man smiled.

"Juliet," he said. "*Juliet* is the sun."

Did the old man listen to Shakespeare in his own language, back in his country that doesn't exist anymore? Is it possible that in his small village, there was a troupe of traveling actors who passed through the countryside every year, performing a different Shakespearean play each time? Is it possible that the old man loved the poetry of William Shakespeare and never missed a performance? Did he crouch as a small boy behind the cloth-curtained stage of the traveling troupe and absorb every word they spoke so that the language of Shakespeare became part of every fiber of his being?

I will never know.

I studied the former olive oil can carefully. This is something you must do when you're an apprentice. You must look at all finished objects with the knowledge that they came from something unfinished, something in an unbegun state. You need to consider all their states of being, all their transformations.

Each cutter had been created in the image of something that already existed: a lantern, a candelier, a candlestick. There was a theme to all three cookie cutters: they were all objects of light, they were all objects that had been most often used in a previous era, they were all objects most often constructed of tin.

The old man wanted me to learn how to find consistency. That was why he taught me by example. That is what it means to be an apprentice to the art of possibility.

A breeze gusted through the trailer and set the cookie cutters jostling and tinkling together. The noise that the cookie cutters made was like the noise of a thousand soda can tops strung together with string and shaken gently. Sunlight glinted off the metal. It was the same kind of beauty that you see in a sunshower, light broken to shards through rain.

Shards. How I love that word.

"There was a time," the old man said, "when most cookies were made with cutters."

The drop cookie is a modern invention, according to the old man. Cookies used to take time and care. They were not beaten together and immediately dropped onto a metal sheet and baked. They were not patted into a pan and called bar cookies. They were mixed, chilled, rolled, formed, cut, baked, dipped, powdered, sprinkled, iced, decorated. They were delicately sugared and a trifle brown around the edges. They were thin, not thick.

"Lemon peel," the old man said. "Always put lemon peel in your sugar cookies."

You wouldn't think that the old man would have known that much about baking. To look at his Jewell's shopping list you would never have guessed that the old man was a master cookie baker.

It's possible that the old man once baked sugar cookies with lemon peel for someone he loved, back when he lived in his country that doesn't exist anymore.

Did Tamar ever do anything like that?

I could come right out and ask Tamar some of my answer-demanding questions, such as, "Did you ever bake cookies for someone you once loved, such as my father? What is my father's name? Where did you meet him? Where is he now? Did he love you, and did you love him more than words can say?"

But I don't.

"How did you get pregnant?" is what I ask.

Tamar doesn't mind questions that sound scientific. She likes science, except when it runs amok as in the case of margarine.

"In the usual way," Tamar said.

Tamar knew what I was really asking. I was asking about my father. I was asking about love.

I should have asked the old man.

There's a chance that when the old man was seventeen and still living in his village that doesn't exist anymore, he fell in love. People grew up fast in the olden days. By ten you could be considered close to an adult. When the old man was a young man, fifteen or sixteen, did he meet a girl? Was she a girl that he had grown up with but had never noticed until she was a young woman with brown curls and he was a young man?

He saw her one day, walking down the road in the spring wearing a dress with yellow flowers printed on it, running upstairs to the stone house above the bakery where she lived with her family.

She was a graceful girl. She was singing, or humming, as she ran up the stairs. She was wearing brown leather sandals. The smell of yeast rising in the bakery below her home came to the young man's nose, and he breathed in and watched her run and listened to her humming.

Did the old man foreverafter associate the smell of baking bread with the image of a pretty, running girl?

When she got to the top of the stairs the young girl sensed something, and turned around, and saw the old-man-as-a-young-man. She met his brown eyes with her own. She looked right back at him. She knew his name.

She whispered it to herself: *Georg*.

She smoothed the skirt of her dress with the yellow flowers printed on it. She was just about to push open the door of her home—her mother had left it ajar for her—and her hand was suspended in the air while she gazed back at the young man. She stared for a moment, maybe two seconds, then laughed and pushed her hand at the air and opened the heavy wooden door and disappeared. The old man stared for a few minutes more and said her name to himself.

What was her name?

Was it Juliet?

*Juliet*, he might have thought. The sound of her name, unspoken, hung in the invisible air before him. *Juliet, Juliet, Juliet*.

Did the young Georg make cookie cutters for Juliet? Did he make her beautiful objects that were also useful? Did he bake sugar cookies for her and teach her the secret of adding lemon peel to the batter?

When I first met the old man I dreamed up a life for him, back in his country that doesn't exist anymore. His father, his mother, his younger brother Eli, all of them living together in their warm thatched hut, cornmeal mush or hot gruel for breakfast, a black iron pot of stew for dinner, the mother beating clothes white against the rocks, the father teaching his sons the art of the forge, how to turn heated metal into objects of use and beauty. I dreamed of the old man as a hero, rescuing tiny babies from floodwater, surviving ten years of unjustly sentenced solitary confinement.

Before he was gone I learned more about the old man's real life, but not all. You can't ever know all there is to know about a life. There will be gaps.

There may well have been a girl named Juliet. It's possible. She may have lived and breathed in the old man's village. The first time the old man ever saw that girl, she may have been running up the steps above the bakery, wearing a dress printed with tiny yellow flowers. Maybe the old man never forgot the sight. Maybe the old man thought of her every day of his life. He might have loved her more than words can say.

My only hope is that she loved him, too.

# Chapter Eight

One day last fall Tiny pulled up to CJ's trailer just as CJ's white Camaro screeched off the road, up over the grass, and around the bus. The top was down. There was a man in a red flannel shirt behind the wheel. He gave Tiny the finger.

"Jesus H Christ," Tiny said.

I looked over at CJ. There was a look on his face.

"Who's that driving your car, CJ—your dad?" one of the North Sterns boys said.

"Yeah, is that the famous Chucky Luck?"

"No that ain't my dad," CJ said. "I told you about my dad. Does that guy out there look like a professional wrestler to *you?*"

The boys looked out the window.

"I guess not."

"Well there's your answer," CJ said.

"How about your mother? Is she a professional wrestler too?" one of the boys said.

Everyone was quiet. No one talks about CJ's mother. CJ Wilson's mother has never been seen that I know of. Were it not a law of nature, you might wonder if CJ even has a mother. CJ looked at the boy who asked the question. The boy looked right back at him.

"I'm asking about your mother, CJ."

CJ turned around and pointed to me.

"And I'm asking about Wipe's father. Wipe? Where's your father at?"

All the boys turned and looked at me. The boy who asked about CJ's mother laughed.

"Maybe he ran off with CJ's mother."

"Yeah. CJ's mother and Wipe's father!"

CJ looked at me while the boys laughed. Didn't say a word.

There must have been something CJ's mother loved about CJ's father. There must have been something Tamar saw in my father, something she loved, even though she won't talk about him. CJ may well wonder about his mother the way I wonder about my father and grandfather.

There was a time when I would have given anything to know about my grandfather, Tamar's father, that man living the life of a hermit in a patch of primeval forest near the Vermont border. I used to ask Tamar about him. One time I asked her when she was rubbing the once-frostbitten toes of her right foot with mineral oil.

"Is your foot hurting?" I said.

"No," she said. She wiggled it in my face, to prove how non-hurting her foot was.

"Do you think, Ma, that a hermit could survive on about fifty dollars a year?" I said.

"Absolutely not."

"How much then? How much do you think a hermit who does all his own trapping and food-gathering would need to survive with just the bare essentials?"

"At least five hundred," said Tamar.

She knows. She always has an idea.

"Why five hundred?"

"Food staples. Candles and waterproof matches. The occasional tool. One Greyhound bus ticket per year. Books."

Books. Would a hermit read books? Is that something a hermit would do?

"Are you sure about the books?" I said.

"All hermits read books."

"But he wouldn't have to spend money on them," I said. "He could hike into the nearest village and use the library."

"He could not use the library. To use a library, you must obtain a library card, and to obtain a library card you need a permanent address. A hermit does not have what would be considered a permanent address. Also, a hermit would not return to a village often enough to avoid huge overdue fines, which he could not afford to pay."

She made sense.

"A bus ticket?" I said.

"All hermits must leave their hermit dwellings once a year. It's an unwritten rule among hermits. It's part of the Hermit Bill of Rights. As a hermit expert, I would've thought you already knew that."

I took my roll of adding-machine paper and started out of the kitchen.

"Don't be mad," Tamar said.

"Then don't humor me. Good-bye."

"Where are you going?"

"To visit a friend."

"Which friend?"

"Georg Kominsky: American Immigrant," I said.

"That's seven miles, Clara."

"It's early in the day," I said. "I'm a good walker. I'll be there by lunchtime."

I put my roll of adding-machine paper in its tin holder and zipped it into my backpack.

"Be careful," Tamar said. "Watch for cars."

Do not ever walk seven miles in sandals without socks. I knew this before I was half a mile down Route 274 but I did not turn back. I refused to give Tamar the satisfaction. By the time I was at the intersection of Crill Road and 274 my feet were not in good shape. I took my sandals off and wound dandelion leaves around my toes so that they would stop rubbing up against each other. Every quarter mile or so the dandelion leaves would grind themselves into a pulp and I had to wipe them off and start over again. After a while blood from the blisters started mixing with the green dandelion leaf pulp. I wished desperately that it was fall, so that the milkweed pods along the road were ready to burst, and I could line my feet with the silky down inside them. For the last three miles I dreamed about the softness of milkweed in the fall.

The old man was working in his onion garden when I got there. By then I was barefoot, despite the possibility of rusty nails and broken glass on the road.

"Clara?" he said.

"It is I. Do you have a Band-Aid?"

"Yes."

He got up and went into his trailer. The minute he said "yes" tears started coming out of my eyes. I sat down on the floor in his miniature bathroom and he handed me a tin box of Band-Aids. The box had a hinged lid. It was unlike the flimsy paper box of Band-Aids that we have at our house.

"This is a very nice Band-Aid box," I said.

I picked out two large Band-Aids, two narrow small ones, and two round ones.

"This box is a metal object, and it is also useful," I said. "But is it beautiful?"

"Why aren't you in school?" the old man said.

"Why aren't I in *school?* It's summer vacation. Don't you know *any*thing?"

I heard myself say those words. They came popping out. They hung in the air between us. They ran like subtitles in the bottom of my brain: don't you know *any*thing? don't you know *any*thing? don't you know *any*thing?

The old man knelt down on the floor beside me. He unrolled some toilet paper and wadded it up and passed it to me. I did not say, *I'm sorry.* What would be the point? When words like that come out of your mouth they cannot be reclaimed. They already exist. They're in the world for the rest of your life and nothing you can ever say will take them away.

People are like that, too. Even if they die moments after they're born, they existed. They were alive. The memory of them can never be taken away.

I took the toilet paper and wiped my eyes. The old man pulled my sandals off.

"These are not good shoes for walking," the old man said.

I said nothing. I kept my silence. I forced myself not to say the words that were shouting themselves inside me: *don't you think I know that by now?*

The old man took another wad of toilet paper and wet it in his miniature sink. He dabbed some soap on it and washed my toes. The soap stung but I said nothing. When he was finished, he dried my feet with a white towel and put the Band-Aids on.

"You walked the whole way?"

"The whole way."

I did not put my sandals back on. I looked inside them and saw the reddish stains from my blood on the toetips. We went back outside to the onion garden. The old man grew nothing but onions and onionlike plants such as chives. He used to eat an onion a day. For good health, he said. That's something they did in his village that doesn't exist anymore. Everyone ate the equivalent of one raw or cooked onion every day. Everything they cooked was cooked with onion. Onions have special properties that protect your health. That is what the old man believed to be true.

His breath didn't smell like onion either. You'd think it would, but it didn't. That's because the old man developed an immunity against onion breath. He ate so many onions in his life that they didn't affect his breath. He had an affinity for onions.

In his onion garden there were some onions that came up every year. The chives were the first things up in the spring. You could see them poking their narrow green stalks up before the snow melted, like miniature quills from the olden days. Chives thrive in the cold. They are not intimidated by lingering snow and ice. They are indomitable.

Now that the old man is gone, and his trailer has been crushed into a slab of scrap metal, I wonder if the chives are still there. Do they still live beneath the ground? Will they push themselves up through the last of the snow and ice when spring comes again?

That day, the old man and I sat by his onion garden next to the bank of Nine Mile Creek, near the forge that he bought at the auction in North Sterns, as he wet a rag and wiped the dried blood off my sandals.

"You fought with your mother?"

I said nothing. Awful words chased themselves around the bottom of my mind but I did not let them out.

"Here," the old man said. "Divide this clump of chives."

He gave me a trowel. I used to call a trowel a spade until the old man corrected me. "A spade is a long, shovel-like tool," he said. "You are talking about a trowel."

"Plunge the trowel straight into the center of the chives," he said. "Then work it back and forth until you can lift out half the clump in one trowelful."

I did not hesitate. If I had been on my own I would have, but because I was with the old man I plunged without hesitation. He was the master. I believed in what he said. The chives came out easily.

"That clump is for you," the old man said. "Plant them at home."

"Tamar is keeping my grandfather from me," I said.

The old man took the clump of divided chives from me. He packed some dirt around the roots, wrapped the whole thing in wet newspaper and then put it in a plastic Jewell's bag.

"I have a grandfather out there and Tamar won't tell me anything about him," I said.

"Where is he?"

"He lives in a primeval forest. He's a hermit."

"What is a hermit?"

Sometimes that happened. I forgot that he was an immigrant. I forgot that English was not his first language. I forgot that he couldn't read. He had no idea how to sound a word out, how to go to the dictionary and look it up. The old man couldn't absorb the meaning of a word from the writing around it, the way I do when I read a book. He had to hear it in conversation. Probably several times he had to hear it, before he could even register it as a word he didn't know. Then and only then could the old man start to grasp the possible meaning of a word like hermit.

"A hermit lives in a cave in the woods," I said. "He spends most of his time foraging for basic necessities. The rest of the time he sits and smokes a pipe and thinks."

The old man pulled a large bunch of his scallions. Four or five scallions to the old man were the equivalent of one raw yellow onion. Two walla-walla onions counted as one raw yellow onion. Chives did not really count as part of a raw onion. Chives are ornamentation and flavoring more than anything else, according to the old man.

"So your grandfather is a hermit who lives in a primeval forest," he said.

The old man pulled the large drooping green outer layer of scallion off each of the scallions and tossed them back into the onion garden. The old man wasted nothing. What some people might think of as garbage—the outer layer of a scallion—he viewed as fertilizer for future scallions.

"He might be," I said. "He very well may be. But Tamar won't tell me anything about him."

"So you do not really know where your grandfather is?"

"That is correct. But I think he's a hermit up near Vermont."

"You think."

"I'm *conjecturing*," I said. "It's a definite possibility."

He said nothing. He took his garden hose and uncoiled it, then turned on the water so a thin stream trickled out. The old man did not believe in a hose gushing water. The old man believed in a trickle of water over time, as opposed to a burst of water in seconds. He lay the hose down next to the middle row of walla-wallas. At first the water soaked straight into the ground. Then the ground directly underneath became saturated and the water started trickling down the middle row and spreading into the rows on either side. That was the old man's plan. That's how he used to water his entire onion garden.

"This is a real possibility?" the old man said.

"Of course it's a *real possibility*," I said. "Why do you talk that way anyway?"

The old man wrapped the scallions in more wet newspapers.

"I'm sorry!" I said. "Forgive me!"

Exclamation marks kept stabbing out into the air after the words that I didn't want to let out. Stab and stab and stab, words and more hurtful words pushing against each other inside me, dying to get out.

"Clara."

Then I could stop. The sound of the old man's voice saying *Clara* started running through my mind instead. *Clara clara clara clara clara clara clara*, chiming like a bell.

"Come here," he said.

*Clara come here, Clara come here, Clara come here.*

I followed him. He went into the trailer and lifted a cookie cutter in the shape of a star down from its hook and put it in his shirt pocket. He carried the wrapped scallions in one hand and he held out his other hand to me. I did not allow myself to think that there might be some kids from my class at Sterns Elementary in town, buying candy at the drugstore or a cone at the Woodside. I did not allow myself to imagine what those kids from my class might think and what they might say if they saw me walking with bare bloody feet into town at age eleven, which is how old I was last summer, holding the hand of an elderly American immigrant who was carrying a bunch of scallions in his other hand.

I took his hand. I walked with him. We went into town.

"Are you hungry?" the old man said.

"I am hungry."

The old man opened the door of Crystal's Diner for me and held it while I went in. I go to Crystal's quite a bit. In addition to food out of cans and jars, Tamar will also readily eat a hamburger and a milkshake. Tamar prefers strawberry-chocolate milkshakes. It's an unusual combination.

Crystal lives in North Sterns, farther out than us, with her nephew Johnny. Johnny's special ed. The old man would call him retarded. Johnny has his own booth at the diner. It's only out-of-towners who ever sit in Johnny's booth. Even they learn fast, because Johnny comes walking up sideways, which is the way he walks, and just looks at them with a sad look. After a while they realize that they're in his booth. They get up and go to a different booth. They take their forks and spoons and knives, their plates and their coffee mugs, their jackets and their purses. They wipe up any water-condensation puddles with their napkins and they take their wet napkins with them, too. They leave the booth perfect for Johnny, as if no one but Johnny had the right to sit there. That's the effect Johnny has on people. One look at him and even out-of-towners want to take care of him. Nobody wants to hurt Johnny. Everybody wants the sad where-is-my-booth look to go away from his face.

Crystal's never had to say a word.

Crystal and Johnny live in a two-person family. I live in a three-person family—Tamar, me, and Baby Girl—although Tamar would disagree.

Tamar would say, "It's you and me, kiddo. Get it through your head."

Johnny Zielinski was in his booth coloring in a coloring book. You might think that because he's fifteen, Johnny's too old for a coloring book. You would be wrong. Coloring helps to improve Johnny's coordination, which is not good. He falls quite a bit. He has a hard time with a pen or a pencil, so Crystal keeps a mug filled with giant crayons in his booth. Johnny will color for an hour or more at a time. Many's the time I've watched him.

"Hello, Mr. Kominsky," Crystal said. "Hello, Ms. Winter."

"It's not *Winter*," I said. "It's *winter*. Lowercase w."

Crystal gave me a look.

"And how do you know I was saying it with an upper-case w?" she said.

"I can tell."

"You're right. I did say it with a big W."

"I know you did."

Crystal said nothing about my bare feet, which were covered with Band-Aids but still oozing blood.

"Mr. Kominsky?" Crystal said. "Do you prefer your name spelled with a lowercase k?"

"He doesn't care," I said. "Big K is fine."

"I was asking him," Crystal said.

"Big K is fine," the old man said.

How would he have known? How would the old man have had any idea whether a big K was fine? He couldn't see the words scrolling by in the bottom of his head the way I can. He had no idea what the difference between a big K and a little k is. All he could do was listen for the difference, and the listening difference without the seeing difference is so tiny as to be naught.

We sat down in the booth next to Johnny's booth. He was coloring with a giant red crayon held in his left hand. The old man took the star cookie cutter out of his shirt pocket and put it on the table in Johnny's booth. The sun shone in the window and sparked off the shiny metal. Johnny put down the red crayon and picked up the cookie cutter. He swung it from the tip of his finger. He laughed in his own particular way, which if you didn't know better you'd think was crying.

Crystal brought over two hamburgers and two milkshakes. She set down a bottle of ketchup and a bottle of mustard. The old man gave her the bunch of scallions wrapped in wet newspaper.

"Thank you, Mr. Kominsky," she said. "I will put these to use in the tuna salad."

Was Crystal Zielinski the old man's friend? Did she know he couldn't read? Did the old man love Johnny Zielinski? These are the things I wonder about now that the old man is gone. I remember that day and I wonder.

"Do you love Johnny Zielinski even though he can't read?" I said.

It was a day when I could not stop myself. The words kept flying out of my mouth and there was nothing I could do to stop them. Words that would ordinarily just meander through my mind gathered speed, took wing, and flew into the air.

The old man took off the top of his hamburger bun and squeezed a ring of ketchup around the border of the hamburger. Then he took the mustard and squeezed two drops for eyes and a curved line for a mouth. Then he put the top of the bun back on and mushed the whole thing.

"Do you love me?" I said.

Crystal brought over two glasses filled with ice and water. Johnny clinked his star cookie cutter on the window to see the sun sparkle off it. The old man looked at me.

"Tamar's keeping me from my grandfather," I said. "He's my only family. He's all I have."

The old man gave me his napkin so I could wipe my eyes again.

"Tamar won't tell me about my baby sister," I said. "She will not allow me ever to mention my father. She has no idea how much I need to know."

"Why did your grandfather become a hermit?" the old man said.

That was the old man. That was something he used to do, take what you said and not question it. He just kept on going with what you had told him, as if it were the truth.

"The guilt," I said. "He couldn't take the guilt."

The old man nodded.

"He had to live with the guilt," I said. "Day in and day out, there it was. Wake up in the morning, there it was staring him in the face again."

"And what was it that was staring him in the face?"

"Guilt, because he killed his grandchild."

"I thought it was winter that killed his grandchild."

"Winter played a role," I said. "I do not deny that winter played a role. But who do you think was behind the wheel of that truck? Who do you think was driving when it slid into the ditch? Who was it who decided to go Glass Factory Road instead of Route 12?"

The old man stirred his water with his straw. All the straws at Crystal's Diner are red. Red is Johnny Zielinski's favorite color.

"Everyone knows what Glass Factory Road is like in the middle of a snowstorm," I said. "You don't go Glass Factory. You take Route 12. Route 12 stands at least a chance of being plowed. Route 12 is the only logical route if you're trying to get to a hospital in a snowstorm. If you take Glass Factory you're doomed."

"And so he became a hermit."

"And so he became a hermit," I said. "Can we go find him?"

"I don't think so."

"Why not?"

There was a mean sound in my voice. I could hear it. The words kept going around in my head: *why not, why not, why not.* Stop, I thought. I said my question again. I took the meanness out of my voice.

"Because you don't know where he is," the old man said.

"He's a hermit near the Vermont border!"

The old man said nothing. I listened to my voice again, going on in my head. *He's a hermit near the Vermont border.* But that was only a story.

Again I had made up a story.

My grandfather was a hermit who lived in a patch of primeval forest near the Vermont border. In the summer he gathered berries and dried them in the sun. He traded pelts for the bare essentials. He wore deerskin clothes that he tanned himself. Over the long winter nights, sitting beside the small fire in his tipi, he chewed the deerskin to make it soft and supple. He cut it with his sharp knife and stitched his clothes together with rawhide threaded through a needle made of bone. His moccasins were reinforced with double rows of stitches.

My grandfather was alive up there. He was living that life right now. I could feel the life he was living. I could feel the silence of his life in the tipi, how he wanted his granddaughter, his only surviving grandchild, to come and show him how to make useful and beautiful metal objects. My hermit grandfather was longing for me. I looked at the old man.

"He's up there," I said. "He's in his tipi."

The old man nodded.

"He could very well be waiting for me," I said. "Tamar isn't always right. No one in the world can be completely accurate one hundred percent of the time. It's a law of nature."

He kept nodding.

"Do you know your grandfather's name?"

"Of course I do."

Knowing names is a point of pride with me. I know not only the first names of people, but I know their last names and any middle names they might have. I know all the names of every kid at Sterns Middle School. It's not hard to learn their middle names. You need only look at the teacher's list. One look is all I need. Once there, never gone. That's reading for you.

"Clifford Winter," I said. "That's his name."

It took many a year for me to glean that from Tamar. It took me years of sneaking in a question here and a question there, years of plotting to ask questions when Tamar would least expect it, such as:

"Ma, what was Grampa's name?"

That stopped her. Tamar didn't even hear the question, she was so stunned by me saying the word *Grampa.* I saw that I had made a mistake. There was a look on her face.

"*Grampa?* Did I just hear you say *Grampa?*"

"Yes. What was his name?"

She was still stuck on the word *Grampa.* She started shaking her head and muttering. I had my notebook ready, but I saw that it was a useless proposition. When Tamar starts to mutter, there's no hope.

"*Grampa?*"

Is it really that strange? When I was born in that truck in the ditch in the middle of the blizzard, wasn't I his grandchild? But Tamar was muttering and shaking her head and I closed my notebook and left the kitchen. When I came back an hour later she was forking bread and butter pickles out of the jar and eating them, one slice at a time.

Many moons later I tried again.

"Ma, what's your father's name?"

"Clifford."

No questions, no looks, no muttering. That one just slipped right out of her.

"What do you want to know for?"

"School. Do they call him Cliff or Clifford? Or Ford, maybe. Would Ford be a possibility?"

"What do they want to know in school for?" she said.

"A genealogy project."

She looked at me.

"Family tree. That kind of thing," I said. "Charts. Diagrams. Ancestors. *Et al.*"

Her eyes narrowed. I kept on talking.

"Cliff? Clifford? Ford?"

Suddenly she looked tired. She gave up. I could tell. I can always tell when she decides to stop pursuing something. A tired look comes over her all at once. It invades every cell of her being, and around her the air slumps, too.

"Cliff."

"Thanks Ma. By the way, I also need the name of my father."

I tried. You have to give me credit for trying. I know it's in there somewhere. The name of my father is in Tamar's brain and there is a way to get it out. I have not found it, but there must be a way. A way must exist.

"You don't have a father."

"Everyone has a father. It's a law of nature," I said for the hundredth time, and then we were back to square one. That was all she wrote.


The old man and I sat in our booth and watched Johnny Zielinski play with the star cookie cutter. He could play with something shiny for hours.

"So that's my grandfather's name," I told the old man. "Clifford Winter."

Crystal poured more coffee into the old man's coffee cup. "Cream?"

"Thank you," he said. "Do you have a telephone book?"

She brought it over. The old man slid it across the table to me.

"What's this for?"

"Look in it," he said. "Look in it for Clifford Winter."

I couldn't breathe right. I kept trying to take a deep breath but the air wouldn't go all the way in.

"He's a hermit," I said.

The old man said nothing. I opened up the phone book to Utica, to a page with Clifford Winter on it.

*Winter, Clifford    1431 Genesee Street    732-7953.*

"You can call him," the old man said.

I kept looking at his name in the phone book. Had it been there the whole time? My grandfather, who chewed deer hide to make it soft enough to slip his bone needle through, who traded pelts for salt and sugar and coffee, who collected only dead wood for his campfires, lived at 1431 Genesee Street and had a phone?

"It's not the same person," I said.

The old man carried our dishes to the counter and passed them to Crystal. When he came back, he had a tinfoil gum wrapper in his hand. He started to fold it into a tiny animal, for Johnny.

"My grandfather is a hermit," I said. "It's possible. My grandfather could just as easily be a hermit as you could be an immigrant who lives in a trailer in Sterns and doesn't have any family."

Words, words, terrible words. They kept tumbling out of my mouth. My chest hurt. There was a feeling of despair in my rib cage. Nothing of the person I wanted to be was coming out in my words. The wrong words kept bubbling and churning inside me, that whole long day. My hermit grandfather started slipping away from me, fading north into the Vermont woods. In my mind I reached for him, but he shook his head.

Meanwhile the image of a man I didn't know, sitting hunched at a table in the kitchen of a Utica apartment I'd never seen, started taking shape. Terrible words that hurt the old man kept spilling from my mouth, and Johnny Zielinski was laughing but it sounded like crying.

# Chapter Nine

There is much I still wonder about the old man. Questions I have that I did not have the chance to ask. What did he eat on the ship to America, for example? Was there food on board or did they have to bring their own? Did they eat hardtack and drink water from big wooden barrels belowdecks? Did the ship have a rough crossing? Did it hit a small iceberg and almost plunge beneath the surface of the waves, like the *Titanic?* Where did the young Georg Kominsky go when they finally let him through at Ellis Island? Did he sleep on the street? Was there anyone in New York City who could speak his language? Was anyone nice to him?

They never found out. His parents must never have known what happened to their sons. There were no other children. I know because the old man told me when I was doing his oral history.

"My parents. Myself. My brother, Eli."

That was it, the four of them. Georg, seventeen, and Eli, eleven. They probably told the old man to take care of Eli on the journey. To watch over him. Keep him safe. If they were religious, they probably said prayers every night: God, keep our children safe. But they never knew. *What happened*, they asked themselves. On their deathbeds they were probably still wondering. *What happened?*

Georg's family may have written to the authorities in America.

*Dear America, We have not heard from our beloved sons Georg and Eli. Have you heard of them? Are they alive? Georg's identifying characteristics are these: he is seventeen years old, he has a slight limp in his left leg from a fever he had at age nine, he works well with tin and other forms of sheet metal, especially making decorative lanterns, and he writes in the air with his nose. Eli is eleven. A child. Please help us. They are our children and we are missing them terribly.*

I asked the old man about it once.

"Did your parents write to you after you came to America?" I asked.

"No."

"Why not? Didn't they miss their children?"

"No."

"Then why not?"

"They were dead," the old man said. "They died before I came to America."

He got up and took one of his extralong fireplace matches out of its extralong box and went to the furnace and lit it. He blew the match out and looked at me.

"Don't worry, Clara," he said. "It's all right. They died long ago."

My dreams of the old man's mother and father—the mother in her apron, the father bent at his forge—shimmered in front of me and faded away.

"It was T.B.," the old man said. "Many people died of it then."

I knew about T.B. Consumption. When you're near the end, your eyes sparkle and shine and your cheeks burn red. To the unschooled, a person near death from consumption might look like the picture of health.

"It was soon before we left for America," the old man said. "With both of them gone we decided to leave."

The old man stacked the dishes in his sink and ran hot water over them. He squirted in a little dish soap. Miniature bubbles rose from the steam and then popped.

"My mother used to sit in the bedroom with Eli," he said. "I remember her as a young woman, with Eli a baby. She sat in the dark, singing him to sleep. That's how I like to remember my mother: the sound of her voice in a dark room, singing."

The old man taught me to seek consistency. "Consistency is a part of the art of possibility," he said. "Everything is related to everything else." That's what he was training me in. I wasn't far along in my apprenticeship when suddenly he was no longer there. I was only a beginner. It takes years, many years, to become a master. That's why I'm starting to think that the old man was a child prodigy. He may well have been a prodigy in his hometown. He may well have been the first child in the world to master the art of metalworking at such a tender age, the age of thirteen or fourteen.

It's possible. Think of all the Dalai Lamas, discovered at the age of three or four or, at most, five. There are certain signs you look for. There are rituals and secrets that only this child, the future Dalai Lama, can divine. He can't be taught how to be the Dalai Lama. He can only be born into it. It is his destiny.

I started looking for relationships that would explain my destiny, and the destiny of Baby Girl. That's what the old man taught me:

"Everything is related to everything else. Consistency is a part of the art of possibility."

There's got to be an explanation somewhere. It's hard to know what to look for, though. How do you figure out destiny?

Every week the old man and I baked a different kind of cookie. The rules were few but always consistent; our cookies were (a) rolled, (b) thin and crisp, (c) fully baked. Sugar cookies, gingersnaps, lemon cookies, and the like. We tried out all the cookie cutters. All worked perfectly. All were beautiful. All were constructed from cast-off materials. These were the consistencies among the cookie cutters, and their relationship one to another.

"I'm studying the art of possibility," I said to the old man. "I'm looking for consistency."

"Good," he said.

"Consistencies among cookie cutters, snow, twins, and babies dying in winter."

The old man looked at me.

"Are you sure you understand what consistency means?"

"Consistency," I said. "The agreement of parts or features to one another or a whole."

I do that sometimes. I look things up and get the exact definition. You'd be surprised how many definitions there are for a single word. Take an ordinary word. Snow, for example. Or winter. You would think there would be one, possibly two meanings at most for either of those words. You would be wrong.

"Actually there are several definitions for consistency," I said. "But that's the one I like the best."

"Why?" the old man said.

"Because it means that things fit together," I said. "Things that don't ordinarily go together *can* go together and then the whole will be consistent. It means that there's a reason why things happen the way they do."

"Take a baby," I said. "And take a truck in the ditch. Those are two things that don't ordinarily go together. But if you're looking for consistency you can find it. It can be done."

"How?"

"Well, that's what I'm in the process of finding out. I'm looking for consistency. I'm training my eye to see possibility. Someday the two will mesh."

"And then you'll have your answer."

"In the fullness of time I will have my answer," I said. "That is what I believe to be true."

If I knew for sure that it was Baby Girl's destiny to die, my mind might be eased. If only I had the unshakable belief that she was never meant to take breath in this world. That would be something for me to believe. I could look people in the eye and say, "It was her destiny to be stillborn." That simple statement of fact would answer all my questions. Facts are not arguable. Facts preclude argumentation. I asked Tamar once about this issue.

"Ma, do you believe in predestination?" I said.

"No," she said.

Immediate. Simple. Clear. She didn't have to mull it over for a second. That's Tamar. Tamar is not a muller, nor is she a hemmer or a hawer.

"So what do you believe in then?"

"Luck," she said. "Hard work. Marinated artichoke hearts."

That's Tamar also. Once in a while she comes out with a *non sequitur.* She likes to amuse herself that way. It's a rare occasion that Tamar laughs. A laughing Tamar is an occasion to make the most of.

Later I asked her a follow-up question. That's something that reporters often do. They ask a question, it leads them down another path of thought, and they ask a follow-up question. Sometimes I treat Tamar as if she were the subject and I were a reporter. I used to take notes on my roll of green adding-machine paper, neatly inserted into the paper holder that the old man made for me, but my green adding-machine paper no longer exists. It is no longer part of this world.

Tamar had a strong dislike of my roll of adding-machine paper anyway.

"I hate that thing," she used to say. "I hate its narrowness and its green color. I hate the fact that it's one endless roll. Be like the vast majority of the population, Clara. Use a normal sheet of paper."

I humor her and use my legal pad in her presence. Most legal pads are yellow. Mine is orange. It came from the reject bin at Jewell's. I hate the color orange, but I feel an obligation to the reject bin.

"So, if I understand you correctly," I said, "you believe that luck and hard work, not predestination, determines a person's chances in this world."

"Correct."

"Does destiny play a role in life at all, then, according to you, Ms. winter?"

"Very little if any."

"What about a baby who seemed normal in every regard but who died at birth? Did luck or hard work play a role in this instance?"

Tamar stood up. She headed outside.

And that was it. Sometimes reporters keep on asking their questions and they keep on asking and they keep on, and once in a while their subject screams out the truth, just to shut them up. I hoped that Tamar would do that, too. But she didn't. She never does. On the subject of Baby Girl, Tamar's a closed book.

My baby sister was born with perfect fingers. I know because once I asked Tamar and she answered without thinking. I sprang the question on her. If there were anyone else to ask, I would ask anyone else, but who is there? My grandfather is a sore subject. I know that because that's how Tamar refers to him.

"Sore subject," she said to me when I inquired about him. "Moving right along."

That's another one of Tamar's famous flat statements: *moving right along.*

"Just tell me one thing," I said. "Did she have all her fingers and toes?"

"Who?"

Tamar knows who I'm talking about. Still she pretends ignorance.

"My baby sister. Did she have ten fingers and ten toes?"

"Yes," Tamar said. "She had all her fingers and all her toes. But she wasn't your sister. Your sister is someone who lives with you and grows up with you. That's not what she was."

I didn't answer. I didn't touch that remark. Not with a ten-foot pole. Tamar has all her answers ready. The not-being-a-sister, the what-makes-a-sister and what doesn't. How would she know? Did she ever have a sister?

"Do you consider yourself an authority on sororal relations?" I said.

"Where do you get these words, Clara?"

"Sororal relations is not a word, it's a phrase."

"Where do you get these *phrases*, Clara?"

I gave her a look. I can do it, too, give looks, although I rarely choose to do so. The truth is that I attract unusual words and phrases. They come drifting toward me out of thin air, invisible, and then they sense my presence and quickly attach themselves to me. That's because I'm a word-person. My first-grade teacher told me that.

"Clara Winter," he said. "You are a word-person and don't ever forget it."

He was right. He knew. He could tell. It's something that can be sensed. There's a difference between word-people and non–word-people. The old man, he was a non–word-person. Was the old man's mother a word-person? His father?

Who knows?

It all comes back to the truth, and what the truth might be. Still, it's easier to make up a story than to tell the truth. I don't even know what the truth is. Tamar will not answer my questions. She does not even allow me to *ask* my questions. It's a force she exudes. It's an aura that surrounds her. I want to know everything about my baby sister, and everything is what I don't know. There is so much left unasked, so much that can't be answered.

"Was I a premature baby?" I asked Tamar.

Notice how I did not say "were *we* premature babies." Tamar would not have responded if I had used "we." She does not respond to me when I refer to myself and my baby sister as "we." Tamar answers only to "I." I have to phrase everything in the singular, as if it was ever only me, me myself and I, no baby sister twirling and somersaulting beside me.

"A little."

I've done a lot of research. There's a great deal I know about conception and pregnancy and birth, things that Tamar may not even know despite the fact that she has experienced all three and I am but a callow youth.

Can a girl be callow? Or is it a boys-only word?

Tamar is a straightforward person. She believes that knowledge is power. More than once she's told me, *Knowledge is power, Clara. If knowledge is power, then why won't you tell me about my sister?* is my silent response. You can't say that to Tamar though. She's not that kind of person.

Baby Girl may have had undeveloped lungs. She may have been unable to take a breath of frigid Adirondack air even if she had wanted a breath of it.

A baby's heart beats extremely fast. Not as fast as a hummingbird, but far faster than a grown human being's. If you're trying to get a baby's heart going, you have to keep jabbing and jabbing at a baby's chest. I doubt if that's something Tamar knew how to do. This was quite a while ago. This was eleven years ago. They may not have known much back then, about how very fast a baby's heart beats, and about how hard you have to work to keep it going.

Was Baby Girl an old soul? Was she not supposed to be born? Was she accidentally trapped inside my mother's body, a terrible mistake? Do babies have a choice? Do they have the ability to choose to live or die?

$M$y roll of green adding-machine paper used to sit snugly in the holder the old man made for me. I can still see it, even though it no longer exists. When last I saw my roll of adding-machine paper, many notes had been taken about the old man. Most of them I took down when first I met him, when he was my immigrant oral history project. Some of them were about his little brother, Eli.

The day I asked him about Eli, the old man was wrapping tinfoil in the shape of a butterfly around a sweet potato. The old man loved sweet potatoes. He often ate one for lunch.

"Okay," I said. "Why didn't Eli come to America with you? That was the plan, wasn't it?"

The old man pinched the tinfoil butterfly until it had antennae, then he carried it over to the fridge and put it inside next to his quart of Dairylea milk. The old man only bought a quart at a time. It would last him a week unless I put too much in my hot chocolate. Then he ran out and had none left for his coffee. He never said anything though. He just drank it black. I wonder now if the old man hated drinking black coffee, those times when I drank up his milk.

"Wasn't Eli supposed to come with you?"

"It was snowing," he said. "There was a lot of snow."

He got up and went over to the sink and ran some water onto the dishes.

"Snow that was blowing straight into my face. I couldn't see."

I unspooled some more of my green adding-machine paper and wrote on it. *Snow . . . straight . . . couldn't see.* I know about snow like that. The old man drank the rest of his coffee. It had to have been extremely cold by then, but he never wasted anything.

"Was Eli wearing boots?"

I pictured boots, heavy lace-up boots such as they must have made long ago in the old man's country that doesn't exist anymore.

"Yes."

"Did he follow in your footsteps? That's what I did when I was nine and Tamar and I were stuck in the blizzard."

"No."

"Did you carry him then?"

"I left Eli with the lantern," he said.

I held the thickly spread bite of toast under the table, then I put it into my mouth. I tried to swallow it without biting, the way Catholics do with the wafer.

"It was too cold," the old man said. "There was too much snow. It was the dead of winter. I couldn't carry him."

The old man couldn't carry him.

There was too much snow.

*It was too cold. Too much snow.* That was all I needed to hear: *There are many ways to die,* I remembered the old man saying to me, long ago.

I wrote it all down. Then I wound the spool of green adding-machine paper back up. Around and around I went. It took a long time. Then I put it in my backpack. The old man finished wiping the dishes dry, plucked up his damp yellow dish towel, and hung it over the oven door handle. He hung it exactly the same way he always hung it, smoothing out the damp wrinkles.

*Too cold. Too much snow. I couldn't carry him.*

The old man's little brother, Eli, died in the snow. I watched the old man smoothing out the wrinkles in his yellow dish towel. Even if I closed my eyes so that the sight of the old man smoothing his dish towel disappeared, I knew I would still see him. Nothing would ever be the same as it had been minutes earlier. Now everything was different. Now he was an old man who had lost his brother.

The church lights were on across Nine Mile Creek, but they wouldn't be on for much longer. Choir practice was almost over. Tamar would soon be driving up to the entrance of the Nine Mile Trailer Park. The windshield wipers would be on because of the almost-freezing rain, and the broken one on the right would be squeaking. I looked out the window at the church across the creek, trying to see the lights through the rain, but all I could see was a young boy—eleven years old—lying still in the snow, wearing a pair of heavy lace-up boots.

Inside my chest, my heart hurt. It came to me that my whole life long, I would carry with me the memory of the old man standing by his stove, smoothing his dish towel. Up and down, up and down, yellow stripes appearing and disappearing under his hand. Across Nine Mile Creek, the lights blinked out. The old man sat across from me at the formica table that he found on scavenging night, lost in his dark lantern world, unspeakably sad.

Six minutes ticked by, and it was time to go. I folded my jacket over my arm and took two sugar cookies wrapped up in a paper towel, one for me and one for Tamar, for the ride home. I wiped my eyes on my jacket sleeve. It was dark. Tamar wouldn't notice.

She noticed.

"What's wrong?"

"Nothing."

Tamar kept one arm on the steering wheel and one eye on the road. She kept looking over at me. She knew to be quiet. When we drove into the driveway, she leaned across me and unbuckled my seatbelt. She stretched her arm way out and opened up the car door for me. She used to do that when I was a child.

It was cold in the house. It's always cold in the house. I turned up the thermostat to 72 degrees and sat on top of the register in my room. Warm air came blowing up underneath me. It made my hair fly up in the air. It came seeping through the layers of socks and pants and underpants. I curled up with my knees to my chest and lay right on top of the register. Two floors below me, the furnace hummed. I love that hum. Warm air blew around me and through me. I warmed. My muscles started to unclench.

There were footsteps in my room. I kept my eyes closed. I stayed curled up. The footsteps came over to where I lay on the register. Something clinked onto the floor next to my head.

Footsteps receded.

I opened my eyes. Steam curled out of the mug on the floor next to me. I breathed in sharply through my nose, to try to draw the steam over to my nose so I could smell what was in the cup. Tea? Hot chocolate? The steam would not cooperate and drift itself over to where I lay breathing in quickly. I started to hyperventilate from trying so hard to drag it over.

Coffee? Hot mulled cider, which I had once read about in a book?

None of the above.

A mug of hot water, with slices of lemon floating in it. I took a sip. It tasted sweet. Could there be sugar in it? Could Tamar have spooned in some white poison, which is what she's been known to call sugar? I lay back down on the register. Tamar had not turned the thermostat down, she had not said anything to me about wasting energy, she had not told me to put a sweater on if I was cold. Tamar, my mother, had brought me something sweet and hot to drink.

I closed my eyes and tried to let the young Georg drift through my mind, standing on the pier at Ellis Island, drawing stars and stripes in the air with his nose, his dark olden-days coat hanging down on his shoulders.

But he wouldn't stay. He disappeared.

What came to me instead was the old man at his forge, the one he rescued from the auction in North Sterns. The old man stringing aluminum soda can tops together. The old man searching for possibility on scavenging night. The old man making me a lantern that was not a match for my missing lantern earring.

Warm air kept blowing up through the register. I sipped at the hot lemon water until it was all gone.

There's many a time I've missed Baby Girl, missed her terribly. She would have walked beside me in the halls at school. Her locker would have been next to mine, in the last row of lockers where the U-V-W-X-Y and Z lockers are. There're only a few of us at the end of the alphabet. There's not all that many students at Sterns Middle School to begin with.

She would have understood without explanation why I changed the W in Winter to w. That's what twins do. They don't have to explain things to each other. Or maybe the W would have remained uppercase after all. If my baby sister were alive, winter would not have won. Tamar and my grandfather would not have been defeated by a blizzard.

They would have triumphed in the face of adversity.

They would have laughed in the face of death.

My baby sister would have been born, taken her first breath of icy Adirondack air, and screamed. My grandfather would have had no reason to flee to a patch of primeval forest near the Vermont border and become a hermit. There would be only one topic to avoid with Tamar, and my sister and I, together, would have insisted that she tell us about our father. Helpless against the mysterious power that twins together exert, she would have agreed.

Perhaps Tamar would choose to eat foods not necessarily jarred or canned. She might like not only marinated artichoke hearts but fresh artichokes steamed and eaten with lemon mayonnaise, such as I once read about in a magazine. Tamar might have allowed more sugar in the house. The three of us—Tamar and her twin daughters—might have baked sugar cookies together.

Everything might be different, if my baby sister had lived.

CJ Wilson might never have looked at me with those eyes. He might never have flipped up my skirt, the first day of school last fall. My chickens might not have turned out mean. There would have been someone to feed them with me, to research chicken violence with. There would have been someone else to love the words I love. Peter Winchell, who has a locker next to mine, would be the person who was supposed to have a locker next to mine, instead of being a boy taking away a locker belonging to someone else, someone he's never met, someone the school never heard of, someone no one besides me has ever known and no one besides me has ever dreamed about, a ghost girl: my sister.

# Chapter Ten

It was the old man's idea that I go to Utica and seek out my grandfather. We were at Crystal's Diner. It was a Wednesday afternoon, and instead of going home after school I had walked to the old man's trailer. I used to do that sometimes. I was taking notes on my roll of adding-machine paper, which I started keeping at the old man's trailer when it continued to irritate Tamar.

"The very sight of that damn green thing annoys me, Clara," Tamar had said, one time too many.

The old man was stirring cream into his coffee and watching Johnny Zielinski play in his booth. Crystal brought Johnny a plate of french fries and a little bowl of ketchup—red, his favorite color—to dip them into.

"Now, how close was your father's forge to your house?" I asked the old man.

I was asking a series of questions for *Georg Kominsky: American Immigrant* and I wanted to get the details right. Take a fake book report for example. You have to get the details right, otherwise who would ever want to read the fake book?

The old man looked at me.

"My father's forge?" he said.

Then I remembered. I had made the whole story up. It was all a figment of my imagination. It's hard to get away from things once they're written down. Written down, things become real. I had a memory of the old man as a child, little Georg, living with his father and mother and his baby brother, Eli, in a hut next to a forge, in their town that doesn't exist anymore. Georg and his father, every morning eating their cornmeal mush and heading out the door for a day's work. Georg the apprentice, his father the master.

None of it existed.

None of it was true.

"My father's forge?" the old man said again. "What are you talking about, Clara?"

"Nothing," I said.

He watched me tear away the part of my roll of adding-machine paper that had the made-up story notes on it. I rolled it into a tight tube and then I folded the tube over onto itself. Then I put it into my mouth and chewed.

"Clara?"

I shook my head at the old man. The paper wouldn't chew. It just got soggy in my mouth. There was a taste of paper throughout my entire nose and mouth. How do spies do it?

"Clara."

The old man couldn't read anyway, so I took the paper out of my mouth and threw it into the trash behind the grill. Crystal watched but she didn't say anything. I pictured the old man the night I first saw him, hanging lanterns in Nine Mile Woods.

"What will happen when you're gone?" I said to the old man.

It was happening again. Words, tumbling out of my mouth without heed.

"Like if you move away or something?" I said.

Too late. The old man already knew whereof I spoke. He already knew I was looking ahead to the day when he wouldn't be there, to the day when he would be gone.

"Clara."

*Clara clara clara.*

"It happens," I said.

He said nothing.

"Everyone will be gone," I said.

"You have your mother."

"I want my grandfather. I want my sister."

The old man regarded me. That's the term for a certain kind of look.

"It's true that I will be gone someday," he said. "So will Tamar."

"I know," I said. "I know. That's what I'm talking about."

"But by then you will have found something, Clara," the old man said. "You will have found the one thing that will change everything, the thing that will make sense of your life and keep you going."

I asked Tamar about my father once, point-blank. *Is my father dead?* I asked her. *For all intents and purposes,* she said, which is a typical Tamar response. *Where does he live if he's dead only for intents and purposes?* I asked. *As far as I'm concerned he doesn't live anywhere,* she said, which puts him in the same category as my hermit grandfather, who may or may not be living in a patch of primeval forest near the Vermont border. I kept on, though, and finally Tamar caved in just to make me stop talking.

"Your father was someone I met one night at a party," she said. "The next morning he drove to Virginia and I never saw him again."

She made her eyes huge and stared back at me.

"There," she said. "Does that answer your question?"

"Yes and no. What was his name?"

"He didn't have one."

"Everyone has a name."

"I have no idea what it might have been."

"Is he still alive?"

"No idea."

"Did he know about me and my sister?"

"You mean did he know about *you*," Tamar said. "You don't have a sister."

"Did he know about me?"

"What do you think?"

She stared at me and didn't blink. That's another of her skills. Tamar can go a long time without blinking. It's very difficult to go without blinking. Try it. I didn't answer her question. Answering questions gives the question-asker the upper hand. That's what I wanted to avoid. So I just repeated my own question.

"Did he know about me?"

That's the kind of thing I've learned to do just from observing Tamar.

She shook her head. "Your *biological father* does not know about you. He has no idea about you. I doubt he even remembers meeting me, and therefore it is as if he does not exist."

She stabbed an artichoke heart with her fork.

"Got it?" she said.

She stuck the fork in her mouth.

"Got it," I said.

Then I cleared my plate and scraped it into the wastebasket and put it in the sink. I threw my napkin into the wastebasket. I put my glass of milk into the fridge for breakfast tomorrow morning.

"Good night," I said.

Then I left the kitchen. I went outside and started down the dirt road. The daisies were nodding on their long stems. The Queen Anne's lace was standing tall, with the tiny black dots in the center of each that always make me think of bugs. Queen Anne's lace is not native to North America. It came from another country. It's an immigrant plant.

"And that's all she wrote," I said to the old man. "So as far as I know, my father is alive and living somewhere in this world."

"Then there's still a connection. You have a connection to your father."

If you are ever close to someone in the world, then there exists an invisible connection between you and that person, a connection beyond the ken of ordinary people. I read that in a book about reincarnation and near-death experiences. It's a true book. I didn't make it up. I told this to the old man once and he nodded. He believed it, too.

Tamar? Not a chance.

"Ma? What do you believe happens when you die?"

"You're dead, that's what happens."

"But at the exact point of death, what happens? Where does your spirit go?"

"In the ground, along with the rest of you."

That's Tamar. I knew I could count on an answer like that, and that's the answer I got. Still, I persisted. It's my nature to persist.

"What about the white light?" I said.

"What white light?"

"The tunnel of white light that envelops your spirit. The people you loved who come back to help you from this world into the next."

"Oh, that white light," Tamar said. "That's just the last neurons popping off in your brain. Pop, pop, pop. It's like a camera flash."

"Then how do you explain the many documented cases of eerily similar near-death experiences?"

"I don't," she said.

That's another thing about Tamar. She feels no need to explain or excuse. That's why you can't argue with her. You run into a brick wall. Any time she senses the presence of Baby Girl, for example, the wall appears.

"Ask your mother about your grandfather," the old man had told me.

"You don't know Tamar," I said. "She is unaskable."

"Ask anyway," he said. "You have nothing to lose."

I could feel the truth in what he was saying. I had nothing to lose. The other half of that sentence is *and everything to gain.* My third-grade teacher was fond of that saying. "Children, you have nothing to lose and everything to gain." She made that saying fit a variety of situations, situations that you wouldn't ordinarily think it would fit, such as putting plastic bread bags over your shoes before you put your shoeboots on.

A few days later I tried to ask Tamar about my grandfather. She was eating her dinner, which was the dinner I had made. If I make dinner, she'll eat whatever I make. Even if it goes against her personal rule of cans and jars, she'll eat it: green beans, chicken surprise, and corn pudding. I read how to make corn pudding in a recipe book in the library. In my corn pudding recipe, there is a consistent relationship among all the ingredients.

*One* can of creamed corn, *one* can of regular corn. *One* cup of sour cream, *one* stick of butter. *One* package of cornbread mix. I like that kind of recipe—all the ingredients in a ratio of *one* to *one*—because it means I never have to write it down.

Did the pioneers write down their recipes? They did not.

"So," I said.

I could see Tamar's face get a look on it. She could tell that something was coming, just from the way I said "So."

"So," I said again.

I thought of the old man. *Ask her about your grandfather anyway,* the old man had said. But I couldn't.

CJ Wilson may sometimes ask his father, Chuck Wilson Senior, about his mother, or CJ's mother may be a forbidden topic in the Wilson trailer. Still, there must be times when CJ thinks about his mother, wonders where she is and if she is still living somewhere in this world. CJ might dream about his mother, at night when he's asleep on the pullout couch in the living room of his trailer, which is where I imagine him sleeping.

"Clara, would you clear the table, please?" Tamar said on a Tuesday night the week after the old man told me I should ask her about my grandfather. "It's court night. Chuck Wilson's done it this time."

That was uncharacteristic of Tamar. She does not discuss the dealings of the court with me.

"Second DWI with a suspended, doing 70 in a 25 zone, totaled his Camaro. Plus a resisting arrest and attempted battery of a police officer. State trooper," she corrected herself. "Which is worse."

"What does that mean?"

"Six-month minimum. And the state'll get his kid, I guess. Do you know this boy, Charles Junior Wilson?"

"No," I said. "Never heard of him."

I did know CJ Wilson the chicken, though. I knew that chicken inside and out. I could sense the soul of CJ Wilson, the chicken, emanating from the broken-down barn. Sometimes at night, last year, when the old man was still in his trailer in Sterns and my chickens were still scratching and pecking in the broken-down barn, I lay awake at night and thought about them. I told no one, though. Those chickens were my secret. I said nothing about CJ Wilson the boy, either. Never once in our time together did I ever mention CJ Wilson to the old man.

Tamar was annoyed by the lack of eggs from my chickens. There were still only a few eggs, the ones that I could reach in and grab from outside the pen.

"Clara! When are we going to see some more eggs out of those girls?" Tamar had started to ask.

"Pretty soon, I guess," I said.

I did not tell Tamar that the barn had started to stink, nor did I tell her that the chickens had gone insane. Even on a twenty-below day, I could smell the barn coming from way across the field. Through the snow I trudged, bearing my heavy buckets of feed and water, just as Laura Ingalls Wilder, Pioneer Girl, would have done.

On court night I watched out my bedroom window for Chuck Wilson. A big man driving a pickup with gigantic tires dropped him off and then backed fast out of the driveway. Chuck Wilson's short hair was flattened down on his head. I could still see comb marks. His red flannel shirt strained at the bottom of his belly.

Next day, the day after court, CJ reached out and gave me a shove. A sound that could be a laugh or could be a phlegmy cough came out of Tiny. He reached in his half-pounder M&M bag on the dashboard and selected three red ones. There's a story that he keeps dirty pictures underneath his candy bag. It's possible.

I said nothing. I sat tight on a green vinyl seat next to Bonita Rae Farwell, a North Sterns girl. The North Sterns girls are quiet most of the time but loud when they have to be. They know how to talk mean. They know how to handle the boys; some of the boys are their brothers.

Those girls would not worry about being murdered by a flock of insane chickens. This is what I believe to be true.

From the back I noticed that CJ's head was shaped like a bullet. His dusty dark hair was shaved close to his scalp, with a few dried lines of blood where he got nicked. I once heard him tell the other boys that he and his father took turns shaving each other's heads. In a little while he came swinging down the aisle.

"Wipe," he said. *"Wipe."*

The night before, I had stayed in my room while Chuck

Wilson Senior was in court in the kitchen with Tamar. I did not listen through the furnace duct. I turned on the radio and read *The Long Winter*, by Laura Ingalls Wilder. Thus was I able to ignore CJ on the bus. What you don't know can't hurt you. That's how the saying goes.

Crystal Zielinski heard the old man talking about Clifford Winter who lived on Genesee Street in Utica.

"Utica?" she said. "Do the both of you need to get to Utica, Mr. Kominsky and Ms. winter?"

Crystal stood there with her red dishrag and Johnny's plate of half-eaten french fries. Ketchup smeared like blood.

"Because if you need to get to Utica you can use my truck," Crystal said.

"That would be good," the old man said. "Thank you."

"You're welcome." Crystal took some keys out of her apron pocket. "Be my guest. I just filled it and I won't need it until I close at ten."

Johnny Zielinski loves red so much that even Crystal's truck is red, redder than a fire truck.

"You're a good driver," I said to the old man when we had driven halfway to Utica. He knew how to drive, even though he didn't have a driver's license. Why didn't he? Reading, that's why.

I will keep the old man's secret forever. Nothing will drag it out of me. Even if I'm strapped in a folding chair in the basement of a building with a bare lightbulb shining in my eyes and deprived of food and water and sleep for days on end, I will not give away the old man's secret.

Before I went in to Clifford Hazzard Winter's apartment building at 1431 Genesee Street, the old man asked if I wanted him to come with me.

"No."

"Are you sure?"

"Did the pioneers head westward?"

"Yes," the old man said.

"And that's your answer," I said.

But there was nothing I wanted more than the old man walking next to me down the hallway with the dirty floor and the dark brown paint chipping onto it, and into the elevator that wouldn't go up even when I pressed 6 seven times in a row, then kept my finger on it for a count of fifteen, and then pushed open the stairs door and walked up and around the five flights of stairs to 6.

The old man waited for me outside Clifford Winter's apartment building. He let the motor idle. Only motors and people can idle. It's very rare that you see that word used with anything other than motors and people. If you're a person, you can idle your time away. If you're a motor, you can idle while someone sits behind the steering wheel, drumming his fingers in a rhythm that you can't hear.

If the old man had been with me, I might not have noticed the broken light halfway down the hall. I might not have counted as high as I counted. If you're extremely nervous, you can count. That's a trick that my fourth-grade teacher taught me.

"Class, if you ever find yourself extremely nervous," she said, "try counting. Count as high as you possibly can. If you want, insert 'one thousand' between each number."

That's how I got to be so good at counting exact seconds. It was on the advice of my fourth-grade teacher.

The buzzer next to the door was broken. The cover was hanging half-on and half-off. There was a ripped piece of yellow paper with *C. Winter* written on it stuck on a piece of chewed gum above the buzzer. How do I know that the adhesive was used chewing gum? Because I looked. I looked around that hall for quite a while. The floor was marble. There was a large cobweb high up in one corner of the hall. It was next to the ceiling, where even the tallest broom could not have reached.

I looked at the door across the hall from C. Winter's.

M. Trivieri.

Down the hall: S. Klusk.

Does no one in Utica go by a full first name? Does everyone use initials only? Is this an unwritten rule? I was pondering these questions and lining my feet up perfectly evenly on the dark brown crack between two marble tiles when C. Winter's door swung open.

"What do you want?"

I knew it was C. Winter speaking to me. I turned around and gazed upon him. He looked right back at me.

"What do you want?"

He did not sound impatient, nor did he sound suspicious. He sounded as if he would ask what it was I wanted as many times as it took, until he had an answer. He sounded like Tamar.

"I'm Clara winter," I said.

The air around him became still. If you train yourself, you can learn to sense the quality of the air around someone, how it moves, whether it shimmers, when it freezes. The air around C. Winter had been ordinary air, invisible, bored even, until I told him who I was.

"And you are C. Winter, are you not?"

He nodded. Then one of his eyes started to move. It moved just a little bit. The air around him shook itself, broke apart and started moving again, fast and furious even though he said nary a word.

"May I come in?"

I stood there, waiting. His one moving eye moved a little bit more. Then I was inside his apartment and standing in C. Winter's hallway. I closed my eyes for one brief second and thought of the old man waiting for me outside, down five flights of stairs, the motor idling in Crystal's bright red truck. I stood in the dark hallway of C. Winter's apartment and pictured the beautiful, unearthly red of Crystal's truck.

C. Winter—my biological grandfather—was not a hermit, nor was he a pioneer. He was so unlike what I expected that I became confused in his apartment and had to get out my roll of adding-machine paper so that I could look up the questions I wanted to ask him.

"What's that?" he said.

That was one of the first things that C. Winter said to me. "Notes," I said.

After he asked about my paper roll I could no longer unroll it. C. Winter's eyes were upon my spool of green paper and I couldn't let him see it. You know when there're things you can't do. It's an instinct. Instinct told me not to unroll my adding-machine paper in front of him.

I cleared my throat. I picked up my pen and balanced it between my thumb and my forefinger. If you do that, and then wiggle the pen slowly and curvily, the pen looks as if it's made of rubber. This trick also works with a pencil.

C. Winter sat in his chair. His eyes didn't rest on me the way a hermit or pioneer grandfather's eyes rest on their beloved granddaughter. C. Winter's eyes roamed. I saw them roaming around his living room: the blue chair, the TV that sat on top of a wooden crate, the mattress on the floor. His living room was nearly his whole apartment. Off behind one corner was a small kitchen, called a galley kitchen. Galley kitchens are ship kitchens, small, in which you can stand in one place and reach everything you need. Everything in a galley kitchen is within arm's reach. I learned about this in a book I read on boat-building. It was a real book.

"I admire your galley kitchen," I said. "It must be very convenient."

When I said that to C. Winter, I didn't mean it. I didn't like his galley kitchen, even though it was clean and neat and didn't smell. I didn't like C. Winter's galley kitchen because it was not the old man's kitchen, and all I could think about was the old man's galley kitchen in Nine Mile Trailer Park, with its yellow-striped dish towel hanging over the stove door handle.

C. Winter's eyes kept moving around the room. There are people with eye diseases whose eyes never stop moving. They jiggle back and forth in unison, or one eye roves. It's possible that one eye can remain stationary and the other can rove free within the eye socket. I read that in the medical encyclopedia.

"Isn't it?" I said. "I mean, you can reach everything without having to take a step."

C. Winter's foot started jiggling. Some people have a disease in which their entire body trembles. Every muscle, every bone, all the time. I forget what it's called. The trembling cannot be controlled. Twenty-four hours a day, the victims of this disease live with the trembling.

"Do you ever have to take a step?" I said. "Just a tiny one, I mean?"

"I don't cook."

His voice was a surprise. You don't know that you have voice expectations until the actual voice is there, the sound waves coming at you and entering into your skull, and then you realize that you had expected something entirely different. C. Winter did not sound like what I believe a pioneer or a hermit would sound like.

"Nor do we, except on rare occasions," I said. "Tamar believes that food tastes best when eaten directly from a jar or can."

"Why do you call her Tamar?" he said.

I couldn't answer him. I was already into my train of thought. Words had piled themselves up in my brain and they could not be stopped. They had to emerge in the order I had already given them.

"Tamar, for example, will not eat margarine because she says it's science run amok."

He smiled.

"She always used to say stuff like that."

"She still does," I said.

He was still smiling.

"She still does," I said again. "Tamar says stuff like that all the time. Margarine is science run amok, food should be eaten out of cans and jars, the most ingenious invention on God's green earth is the Swiss army knife."

"That sounds like her," he said. "That does indeed sound like her."

"Don't call her 'her,'" I said. "Her name is Tamar. Everyone's got a name."

He shook his head. His eyes roamed. His knee jiggled up and down.

"Everything on God's green earth has a name," I said. "Or *should* have."

I saw Crystal's bright red pickup the minute I came out of the apartment building where C. Winter, my biological grandfather, lived. I kept my eyes trained on the drumming fingers of the old man the entire time I was walking down through the green-plastic-awning roof over the little slanting tunnel that leads out of the apartment building—in case it rains?—and walking across the parking lot where a few rusty cars and a few rusty trucks were parked. I watched the drumming fingers of the old man sitting behind the steering wheel of the idling truck until I was at the truck itself. Then the old man stopped drumming and let me in.

"Well?" the old man said.

I shook my head. I climbed in next to him and strapped the seatbelt over my shoulder, across my chest, and buckled it. It was too loose. I pulled it as tight as it would go. If I had had access to my emergency seatbelt system I would have hooked it up, but the only place in the world where my seatbelt system exists is in Tamar's car, at home.

Dark gray air hung above us, a winter sky. Across the street there was an A&P store with three shopping carts left in the parking lot.

"Look at that," I said to the old man. "Is it that hard to take a shopping cart back to the store?"

He didn't say anything.

"To the entrance, even? I mean, is it that hard?"

At Jewell's Grocery, no one leaves shopping carts in the parking lot. That's because there is no parking lot. There's only the road, right in front of the store. The old man put his hand on my seatbelt buckle and tugged at it. He untwisted the shoulder belt where it was spiraled behind my neck and smoothed it down. Then he pushed my hair off my cheek.

"Well?" he said.

"Well," I said.

He pulled the lever so it pointed to "D" and put the blinker on. Down Genesee Street he drove, past the Boston Store, past Bremer & Bullock Liquor, past Munson Williams Proctor Museum of Art, and on to the overpass that leads to Route 12 north. I counted three hundred seconds, the way my teacher had taught me, and looked back. Utica lay behind us, with a rim of snowy hills and dark sky above it. We were climbing out of the Mohawk Valley, heading into the foothills.

"Tell me about your grandfather," the old man said.

"That wasn't my grandfather. That was C. Winter."

The old man looked at me.

"They don't use first names in Utica," I said. "They go only by their initials. Did you know that?"

I forgot that the old man couldn't read. He wouldn't have known an initial from a surname. I turned away and looked out the window at Utica in the distance.

I wanted to keep my grandfather, my real hermit grandfather, where he belonged. I wanted him in his patch of primeval Adirondack forest near the Vermont border, living in his tipi, selling his pelts or trading them for sugar and coffee. The bare essentials. I wanted him to be there, alive and well and full of the answers to my questions. Even as I sat in

Clifford Winter's Utica apartment, my true hermit grand-father, the one I had based my fake book report *Tales of an Adirondack Hermit* on, was working quietly in his tipi near the Vermont border. He was even then chewing rawhide, making it soft so that he could cut it and stitch it into moccasins for me, his granddaughter. I asked him a question in my mind, in italics, and sent it winging through the sky toward him.

*Why did you take Glass Factory instead of Route 12?*

My hermit grandfather couldn't hear me. He was too intent on working the deerskin for my moccasins, softening the stiff leather so that the moccasins he was making as a gift for me would fit my feet like flesh and never, never hurt me.

# Chapter Eleven

The night of the fire, it snowed. It was the kind of snow that falls straight down, each flake thick and furry. Silent snow that silences everything it touches. Snow that makes the entire world quiet.

The old man and I were going to make gingersnaps that night. We were moving on, past sugar cookies and into gingersnaps. A true gingersnap is thin and crisp, a dry, light cookie. The opposite of the kind of snow that was falling that night.

"A gingersnap should break cleanly," the old man said. "It should snap."

Hence the name. A name reflecting the purpose, the very sound of the cookie when broken. When Tamar dropped me off at the entrance to Nine Mile Trailer Park, I stood by the sign for a minute and tried to catch snowflakes on my tongue. It's not easy to do. You would think, in a snow falling so thick and straight and heavy, that you would be able to have a mouthful of snow in just a minute or two. Just lean your head back, open your mouth, and let the cold whiteness enter.

It doesn't work that way. I stood with my head back and my tongue out until I saw the lights go on in the church across Nine Mile Creek. Stained glass, throwing stained shadows on the white ground. You could barely see them, through the falling snow.

Across the creek Tamar was practicing with the choir she's never sung in, and in his trailer I imagined the old man laying out the measuring cup, the measuring spoons, the flour and salt and sugar and ginger, everything necessary for making gingersnaps. Former olive oil cans were hanging by the window, waiting for their destiny to be fulfilled.

I can still see them in my mind. I can see the way they swung in the breeze in the summer, when the old man opened all the windows. I can hear the sound the cookie cutters made then, like ice when it freezes on Deeper Lake up in the Adirondacks, pushing against the shore with a sound like broken glass tinkling. I can still see myself on that night, standing at the entrance to Nine Mile Trailer Park, halfway between my mother across the creek and the old man in his kitchen.

When I stopped trying to catch snowflakes on my tongue, I walked up the lane to the old man's trailer. At first I didn't understand the light in his window. It was an odd light, orange. An irregular light. The light from a lamp is not irregular. Then I saw the lady two trailers down fling open her door. A sound in the air around me grew high and loud. Then I knew that the orange dancing light was a fire in the old man's trailer, and the sound all around me was me, screaming.

"Did you see him come out?" I screamed to the lady two

trailers down. She leaned out her door. She had socks on her feet and she kept stepping on one foot, then the other. Her feet will freeze, I heard myself thinking at the same time as I was yelling at her.

"Did you see him come out?"

My voice kept screaming out of my throat. I could hear my throat getting raw just in the sound of my words. The lady hopped to her other foot.

*"Did you see him come out?"*

She frowned. I could see her trying to figure out what I was saying. Then she figured it out and shook her head. Back and forth. She mouthed some words at me. *No. No. I didn't see him.*

She hopped onto her other foot, then she went back inside her trailer. The door was still open. I stood in the old man's yard. I listened for sirens: none.

"Call the fire department!" I screamed.

I wanted to hear those sirens. I wanted the Floyd Volunteer Fire Department to be on their way. I looked across Nine Mile Creek. The church windows were lit up. They were still singing. Did no one see the flames? Did none of them stop their singing and look out the window and see that the old man's trailer was on fire?

My feet were numb. My sneakers were no good in the snow. What I had intended was to get out of the car and walk only on the trailer park road, and then only on the path that the old man shoveled to his steps. That's what I had intended to do.

"Put your boots on," Tamar had said before we got in the car.

"They're wet."

She gave me a look.

"Soaked," I said. "I would catch my death of pneumonia, should someone force me to wear those boots."

I could see her thoughts chase themselves around on her face. *And why are they soaked?* she wanted to ask. *Can this be my daughter, Miss Prepared For All Snow Emergencies, refusing to wear winter boots on a cold winter night?*

*And whose fault is that?* she would've said, if I had told her why my boots were wet. There was no good reason. It was a reasonless situation. I got off the bus, and I saw the drift, and for once my feet just wanted to jump into it.

The church windows were still lit. You could hardly see them because the flames from the old man's trailer had grown so much brighter. The lady came back out on her trailer steps. She had put her boots on and she was carrying a broom. She ran through the snow to where I was standing.

"Did you see him come out?"

She shook her head again. She looked angry.

Then she started beating at tiny flames with the broom, the tiny flames floating from the window. Black and white wisps with a glow of orange coal, drifting down to the snow.

What good would that do?

Then I remembered my roll of green adding-machine paper. I could picture it, lying in its special drawer on the curved wall at the end of the old man's kitchen that was burning up.

Black dots were crawling through the snow when I looked over to the church again. The windows were still bright through the woods, but black dots were crawling in the snow. The biggest dot, the one in front, ran right through the creek and up the bank toward me. It got bigger and bigger. It turned into Tamar, running so fast that she looked like someone I didn't know.

"Did you see him come out?" I screamed at her. "Did you see him come out?"

She came running up to me and grabbed me. She had no jacket or boots. No gloves or hat.

"Did you? Did you?"

Tamar couldn't talk. She was breathing too hard. She bent over in the middle and sucked in air. I hit her on the back. "Did you see him come out?"

How could she? She was practicing with the choir in the church with the lit windows. No one but me knew about the secret patch of clear glass in the stained window in the churchhouse, that if you stood on a chair you could peek through it and see the Nine Mile Trailer Park through the woods. All Tamar could've heard was the sound of singing. She couldn't have heard the snow drifting down. She couldn't have heard the scrape of a match, whatever match it was that lit the fire that was burning down the old man's trailer.

There was fire coming out of the bedroom window now. No one in all the people standing around us now would've known that was the bedroom window except for me. I was the only one who knew the trailer from the inside. I was the only one who knew that behind that window was where the old man slept. I was the only one who knew that my spool of adding-machine paper, which held the old man's life in its curls of words, was trapped in its tin paper holder in the special curved kitchen drawer.

I cupped my mittens full of snow and shoved them against my mouth. Then I jerked away from Tamar and ran into the trailer. My head was down when I ran in, and the snow was white-cold against my mouth and cheeks. Then there was a peculiar feeling on my head. I had never felt that feeling before. I smelled a certain smell and I knew that the feeling was the smell, and that it meant that my hair was on fire. Where was the old man? Where was the special kitchen drawer? Where was Clara winter? I sucked in air through my ball of snow, but there was no more snow. The snow was gone, and fire had taken its place.

# PART TWO

—*Ductility,* the ability to undergo deformation (change of shape) without breaking.

—*Elasticity,* the ability to return to the original shape after deformation.

—*Fatigue Resistance,* the ability to resist repeated small stresses.

From Metalworking

# Chapter Twelve

I asked the old man a question once, on how he would choose to die, and no answer was forthcoming. I repeated my question several times, in several different ways, but the old man never answered. Instead, he posed a question to me.

"Am I guilty?" he said.

"That's not the question," I said.

"But am I?"

"You're on death row!" I said. "You have to choose: lethal injection or electric chair. It doesn't matter if you're guilty or not."

"But am I?"

I gave up. I took the advice given to me by Tamar when asked about Baby Girl Winter: "Give up." No answer to my death row question was to be forthcoming from the old man. He was fixated instead on the question of guilt. Now that the old man is gone, I think about that. I wonder how my question sounded to the old man. I wonder if he thought I was asking him about guilt.

My death row question was the kind of question that

I used to ask during lunch in the Sterns Middle School cafeteria. It was a Clara winter type of question. I once posed a dying question to the entire lunch table, after I found out about the old man leaving his brother, Eli, in the snow. The old man was still alive then.

"Here's a question," I said. "How would you rather die? Burning to death in a fire, or freezing to death in a snowbank?"

They stopped eating to consider.

"That is such a Clara Winter type of question," Jackie Phillips said.

"Burning," one of the other girls said. "It's quicker. Or wait. Maybe freezing."

"Freezing," another one said. "Burning's too painful."

"Yeah," somebody else said. "Definitely freezing. I heard that if you freeze to death it's painless after the first few minutes."

"You just fall asleep. You stop shivering, and you fall asleep."

"First your toes go, then your fingers, then your lower legs, then your forearms, then your thighs, then your upper arms, then your crotch, your stomach, your chest, and finally your head."

"Your head's the last thing to go."

"That's because all the blood goes to your brain, because that's the most important thing."

I betrayed the old man when I asked that question. There's more than one way to betray someone. You can tell a secret about someone. You can let loose something that you know about an old man, something that happened to him, something that the old man did, without ever mentioning him by name, and then that secret is alive in the world, living and growing and being talked about. At the lunch table five girls sat talking calmly about what happens when you freeze to death, without ever knowing that in our town, in a trailer only half a mile from the school cafeteria, there was an immigrant whose little brother had frozen to death. The girls at the lunch table were talking about how Eli had died, and they didn't even know it.

But I did. That's one way you can betray someone.

"Stop talking about freezing to death," I said.

They looked at me.

"Why?" Jackie Phillips said. "You're the one who asked the question in the first place, Miss Clara."

"You haven't even talked about burning to death," I said. "Isn't there anyone who would choose burning to death? That's the martyr's way to die."

They made faces.

"Too painful."

"Yeah. It's a horrible way to die."

"Think of Joan of Arc," I said. "Think of those poor women in Salem. Think of widows in India committing suttee."

They looked at each other. Had they ever heard of Indian widows committing suttee? No. They may have heard of the Salem witch hunts, but they would not have known that the Salem women died by drowning or stoning. Maybe one non-witch was killed by burning to death. But that's something most people don't know. Mention "Salem witch hunt," to most people, and all they think of is being tied to a stake and burned to death.

"It's a fine way to die," I said. "It's a martyr's death. It's the death of someone who sacrifices her or his life for the sake of principle."

"Objection," Jackie Phillips said. "Irrelevant. Freezing's the way to go."

They all agreed. End of subject. On to sloppy joes.

When I asked the girls at the lunch table that question—*if you had to, would you rather die by freezing or burning?*—the old man was still alive. It was an idle question then, but I think about that day now. Now that the old man is dead by fire, I think about it. Every one of the girls chose freezing to death. There was no question. No debate. Burning was rejected out of hand.

But burning is how the old man died. The old man died in a way that was categorically rejected by everyone at the table.

When I was still in the hospital, reading the dictionary with the tissue-paper pages that Tamar bought for me, I looked up *martyr.* It's one of my favorite words because of the way it has four consonants, including one consonant that occasionally doubles as a vowel, in a row which begin and end with the same letter: r, t, y, r. It's unusual to see a word with that particular four-consonant pattern. Try to think of as many as you can. You'll soon see.

> *Martyr. 1. one who voluntarily suffers death as the penalty of witnessing to and refusing to renounce his religion. 2. one who sacrifices his life or something of great value for the sake of principle. 3. Victim, esp: a great or constant sufferer < a ~ to asthma all his life>.*

Martyr is a tragic word, but these days it's become a word of scorn. People use the word *martyr* indiscriminately, but it's a word that should be used with great care. People tell other people that they're being martyrs to make them stop acting put-upon. That is a misuse of the word *martyr*. It hurts me to hear people use such a word in that way. What I want to say when I hear someone call another person a martyr is this: Martyrs are *dead*.

The whole time I was in the hospital I measured time by four-hour segments. That was the number of hours I had to wait until the nurse brought the small paper cup with the pill in it. The pill was for the pain of the burns and the burned lungs. Toward the end of the third hour and throughout the fourth hour, my mind would sharpen. I could feel the edges honing, the blurriness dissolving. It was during that sharpening time that I concentrated on not thinking about the old man.

When they let me go home the nurse with the brown hair that's shorter on one side than the other gave me a balloon.

"Here you go, sweetie-pie," she said.

I said thank you and took the balloon. It was orange. Tamar was waiting by the nurse's station. She was finishing some forms that they had given her.

"Ready?" she said.

I nodded. I was being chary with my words. *Chary* is a word I learned in the hospital, from the dictionary that Tamar brought in for me after I'd been in the hospital a couple of days. It's the kind of dictionary that in the olden days would have rested on a tall wooden stand in a library, the kind of dictionary that pioneers would've consulted in the New England cities they lived in before they headed west. Laura Ingalls Wilder would have loved such a dictionary. It's possible that she would have consulted such a dictionary to write one of her famous school compositions, which were never fake.

"Thank you, Ma," I wrote on my small memo pad. When Tamar gave it to me, I still couldn't talk too well because of sucking in all the burning air. Quickly I got into the habit of writing short notes if I needed to say something. When writing notes is your only means of communication, you learn to conserve language. You become chary with words.

At night in the hospital, after Tamar went home, I read the dictionary.

*Chary. [ME, sorrowful, dear, fr. OE cearig sorrowful, fr. caru sorrow]*
*1. archaic: dear, treasured. 2. discreetly cautious: as a: hesitant and vigilant*
*about dangers and risks. b: slow to grant, accept, or expend <a man very*
*~ of compliments> syn see cautious.*

Do you see what kind of a word chary is? It means something and its opposite at the same time. You can be slow to accept a compliment and slow to expend one, and the word *chary* will fit either side of your personality. You can be discreetly cautious about danger and risk, and at the same time treasure something dear to you. All these meanings are related.

The old man would have been able to see that immediately. The old man was an expert at seeing the relations between things.

They left it to Tamar to tell me. She waited until we were in the car.

"Buckle up," she said.

I buckled up. Then she reached around me and pulled out my safety system. She strapped on the bungee cords and wrapped the other belt around me.

"Ma?" I said. My throat still hurt and my words were whispery. But one word isn't worth writing down. She could tell that I was asking her why she was strapping me into my safety system.

"Ma?"

Tamar started the car. While I was in the hospital she'd fixed the nonopening passenger door. I noticed right away. There was an indentation in it, as if she'd kicked it or taken a hammer with a towel wrapped around it to my door. She's taken towel-wrapped hammers to things before. So the finish doesn't scratch, is what she said. But the door worked now. I pointed to it.

"Thanks Ma."

Her hand moved to the steering wheel as if she were going to push the lever to "D," but she didn't.

"Clara," she said.

I raised my eyebrows. Raised eyebrows give you a look of inquiry. That's something I've noticed. When you're being chary with your words, but you want to indicate interest in what someone is saying to you, if you want to let them know that you want them to keep on talking, then all you need do is raise your eyebrows. It worked.

"Clara," Tamar said, "the old man died in the fire."

No mincing words with Tamar. She is a woman who is naturally chary with her words. I watched her words go scrolling by the bottom of my mind, then I fell. You can fall in a car. It's possible. What happens is that you sag, and if there's not a

complicated system of safety belts and bungee cords to hold
you up, you fall right onto the floor of the car. Right into the
pit.

*The old man died in the fire, the old man died in the fire.*

It sounded like a nursery rhyme.

"Are you sure?" I said. I had to whisper.

She nodded. Her hand was in front of my safety system,
helping to hold me up. Then her arm came around the back of
my head and neck and clamped onto my shoulder. She kept
nodding. Ahead of us the parking lot of the hospital was
scattered with cars. They shone in the sun. It was a shining
winter day, three weeks after they brought me to the hospital
with burned lungs. Tamar's hand came up and tried to touch
my hair, but my hair was gone. Burnt off.

There had been some of it left in the back of my head, but
when I looked in the hospital bathroom mirror I knew that
I should cut it off. I cut it myself, with nail scissors that the
nurse with curly brown hair gave me when I told her my toenails were getting too long. I did not lie to the nurse. My toenails were in fact getting too long, but that doesn't necessarily
mean that you'll be using the toenail scissors that the brown-
haired nurse gives you to cut only your toenails. You could also
use them to cut hair. Why not? Both hair and toenails need to
be cut. The relationship is consistent.

I stood in front of the bathroom and gathered as much of
my leftover hair as I could and then chopped it with the scissors. Nail scissors are not the best kind of scissors to cut hair
with. They don't have long enough blades. You have to keep
sawing until finally all the leftover hair is chopped off.

If you're missing your eyelashes and eyebrows, if for example
they've been singed off in a fire in a trailer belonging to an

old man, then you're better off with no hair on your head either. This is what I believe to be true. Tamar's hand didn't know what to do when it touched the wisps of hair in back of my head, so she put it back on my shoulder. She was still nodding.

"He's dead?"

"Yes."

"Did they bury him?"

She nodded. If someone's buried, they're dead. They're truly dead. It came to me that I had never asked the old man if he wanted to be buried or cremated.

"Did he want to be buried?" I asked Tamar. But it was a useless question. It was a question without an answer. How could Tamar possibly know if the old man had wanted to be buried?

"I don't know," she said.

That's Tamar. She does not lie.

"Where did you bury him?"

"In the Sterns Village Cemetery."

"Does he have a headstone?"

"Not yet but he will. The Twin Churches are raising money to get one for him."

Her hand was still on my shoulder. I felt myself rocking in my seat. You can rock in the front passenger seat of a station wagon. It's possible. But you might not know you're rocking unless your mother has hooked up your safety system and all the bungee cords are holding you in tightly. When you push yourself forward you can feel them pressing against you. That's how you know you're rocking. I kept whispering despite my throat.

"What will his headstone say on it?"

Tamar shook her head. "George Kominsky, I guess."

"*Georg,*" I said. "It's not *George.* It's *Georg.*"

She nodded. She was either shaking her head or nodding, nodding or shaking her head.

"You're just like everyone else," I said. "Aren't you? You don't even know his real name."

She looked at me.

"You don't even know how to pronounce his *name.* For all you care, the old man could have been named Clifford."

Still looking.

"Everyone has a name," I said. "Everyone deserves to have his name pronounced the way it should be pronounced. But people don't know. People don't care."

Her fingers pressed into my shoulder bone and then let go. Pressed and released. Over and over.

"They do, not, care," I said. "And that's the whole problem."

She pressed and released. Her arm made no movement to put the lever into the "D" for drive slot. I know a lot about driving. When it comes time for me to get my permit, I will be a quick study. That's what my fourth-grade teacher used to call me, a quick study.

Tamar wasn't going anywhere. I could tell she was going to sit in the car, with the motor on and me strapped into my safety system, as long as it took. My throat was raw and my words were whispers. Still, she wasn't going anywhere. So I asked my question.

"Did he die because of me?"

There. It was out there. It was a question out in the world now, hanging in the air between us. The words were out of me. They existed on their own.

"He died trying to get you out," Tamar said.

"I killed him, then."

"He died trying to save you," Tamar said.

Then she took her hand away and put the lever into the "D" position. She took her foot off the brake and moved it onto the gas. The cars in the parking lot winked and blinked in the sunshine. It was winter sunshine, too bright. Painful on the eyes.

"We're going home," said Tamar. Then she put on her blinker and we started up Route 12, out of Utica, heading into the foothills.

When I was very young, when I had first thought of my death row question, I had asked it of Tamar.

"Ma, you're on death row. How would you rather die? By electric chair or lethal injection?"

"Neither," Tamar said.

"But if you *had* to pick."

"I don't have to pick," Tamar said. "Therefore I shall not pick."

She never answered my question. I myself have never answered it either. The day I asked it of the old man, I had my answer ready: lethal injection. That used to be my response to my own question. Injection wins out over electric chair any day. It wasn't even a real choice, it seemed to me. But that's what I know now, and that's why I can never ask that question again. It isn't a choice. You don't get to choose.

Did the old man get to choose? That's what I wonder about. When he came up to the trailer, and saw Tamar screaming, and saw the people all holding her by her feet and arms and legs so that she wouldn't go running into the fire after me, did he choose?

The choir director told me that the old man had a plastic Jewell's Grocery bag in each hand. They spilled when he dropped them.

"What was in them?" I asked her.

She gave me a look, but she answered anyway.

"I don't remember everything, but there was a bag of sugar and a can of ginger. A quart of milk, which spilled when the carton broke."

"Dairylea milk?"

"Yes, Dairylea milk," the choir director said. "I remember the orange flower."

Tamar was screaming like a crazed person. She *was* a crazed person. That's what the choir director told me.

"I have never seen your mother like that," she said. "She was literally out of her mind. There was a look on her face that I hope never to see again in my life."

Tamar wasn't around when the choir director told me that. The choir director also brought me a green rubber frog.

"Something to keep you company," she said.

An orange balloon, a green rubber frog. The world of my childhood is behind me, and I have put away childish things, but you can't tell people that.

"We were all trying to hold your mother back," the choir director said. "There were at least six of us holding her down. The next thing we knew George was past us and running up the steps of the trailer."

Not George. *Georg*. But they don't know. They never knew.

How could the old man have been running? His feet hurt him from the frostbite that he got when he was seventeen. If you didn't know the story, you couldn't tell that his feet hurt him. But when you knew the story, and you knew that when he was seventeen he was caught in a blizzard that killed his little brother, and that he had to walk for two days to find his way out of the woods, then you could tell how much his feet hurt him. All his life, his feet hurt him. But no one who didn't know the story would know that about the old man.

The choir director squeezed the green rubber frog. It squeaked.

"Oh, I didn't know it squeaked," she said. "How cute. And then the next thing we knew the window in the middle of the trailer was open, and you came sliding out of it. He must have found you and opened that window and heaved you out."

That window was the bedroom window. The window in the middle of the trailer was the window above the old man's built-in bed with the built-in drawers below. The old man used to lie in his bed and look out the window at the night sky. I know this because three times, Tamar and I drove past Nine Mile Trailer Park before dawn on our way to the State Fair in Syracuse. Each time we passed the trailer park, I looked out just at the right time to see the old man's trailer. Each time, his window was open and the curtains were pushed aside. It was still nighttime. The old man was still asleep. That's how I know that he went to sleep looking out an open window at the dark night sky. It would have been filled with stars some nights. It would have been streaked with lightning sometimes, or invisible through rain. There is a chance that once in a while, the old man would have climbed onto his built-in bed, looked out the window, and seen the heavens pulsing with the Northern Lights.

"And the next thing we knew, there you were. Lying in a snowbank," the choir director said. "We let go. Tamar got to you first."

*And the next thing we knew, and the next thing we knew, and the next thing we knew.* The choir director kept saying that, as if every one of her memories was a surprise to her.

The old man must have crawled through the trailer on his hands and knees until he bumped into me. He would have known it was me by my foot hitting him on his lowered head, or the feel of my hand under his crawling hand, or maybe the smell of burnt hair. That's a smell you can't not know. He must have picked me up, stood up, and pushed me out of the window.

Did he try to crawl out after me? Did he make it up onto his bed and then be overcome with smoke? Or did he just crumple back onto the floor once I was out the window?

The choir director had her arms out like she was directing the choir. While her eyes were still shut I took the green rubber frog and threw it under the bed.

Did the old man hear Tamar screaming my name? Did he know that I was still alive, and that they would revive me? Did he know that even then the Floyd Volunteer Fire Department was nearly there, and that the men would jump out and put the oxygen mask on me and take my pulse and make sure I wasn't dead, and that then the ambulance would come and take me to Utica Memorial, and that Tamar would stay in a chair next to my bed the whole first three days?

That's what the nurse with the brown hair that was shorter on one side than the other said.

"Your mother sat right in that chair for three whole days and nights," the nurse said. "She wouldn't even hardly leave the room to pee."

What I want to know is when they got the old man out. Did the firefighters go in there and try to save him? Did anyone think of the old man?

Mr. Jewell came to see me a few days after I was home.

"I was walking home," he told me. "George's place was on the way so we walked back together. He waited for me to close up, that's why he was a little later than usual. You must've thought he was inside, because we both saw you run on in there."

Mr. Jewell put a paper bag that said "Jewell's Groceries" on the bed next to me. I opened it. A can of ginger, a can of tuna, a bag of egg noodles, a small spiral notebook.

"When George saw you run in there, he started running too," Mr. Jewell said. "He dropped his bag and they all spilled out."

A spiral notebook? I took it out and turned it over. Red, flimsy, flip-top. Fifty miniature lined pages.

"I wanted to give them to you," Mr. Jewell said. "I know he was your friend."

"Thank you," I said.

After he left I picked up the little spiral notebook again. Why did the old man buy it? What did he plan to do with it? I will never know.

I thought of things that weren't going to happen anymore because the old man was gone, such as biscuit baking. I had told the old man my pioneer recipe for biscuits. Pioneers carried their recipes in their heads. I know this because I once wrote a report on pioneer cooking. It was a true report, I researched pioneer recipes in the Utica Library. It's hard to find pioneer recipes; they were passed down mother to daughter. Daughters learned by observing and practicing. They were apprentices to the art of cooking.

*Take some flour and cornmeal and rising and some good fresh lard if you have it. Rub it between your fingers till it's crumbly. Add some salt. Cut into rounds. Bake, covered.*

"'Rising'?" the old man said. "Baking powder, that must be."

"Must be," I said.

"And lard. We used to use that. That was all we used to use. That, and butter."

He sifted even though I told him not to.

"Did the pioneers sift?" I said. "They did not. They had to pare down to bare essentials before they headed out west. Was there room in a covered wagon for a sifter?"

He said nothing.

"There was not," I said. "A sifter is not a bare essential. You shouldn't be using one."

The old man got a stick of butter from his miniature refrigerator.

"Halt!" I said. "Did the pioneers have butter?"

The old man started cutting butter with two knives.

"Nay sir, I think not!" I said. "Where's the good fresh lard?"

He smiled at me. That was rare from the old man. Smiles were not his forte. The old man finished rolling out the dough, then he took one of his three water glasses and pressed it into the dough. Each round he placed on a pan that he had already greased. They didn't take long to bake. They would have been much harder to bake over an outdoor fire. You wouldn't be able to regulate the temperature. You'd have to use a regular frying pan with the lid on it. They'd be burned on the bottom and maybe underdone on the top. That would be an authentic pioneer biscuit, I thought. Not a perfect round biscuit.

Still, the pioneers would love their biscuits. After a day in the open air, walking behind the wagon in the tracks left by the wheels, or riding one of the ponies off to the side, or leading the cow by its halter, those biscuits would have been delicious. Nothing would taste better than an authentic pioneer biscuit, baked in a frying pan over an open fire. There would have been no leftover biscuits in a true pioneer camp.

The old man was the master and I was his apprentice. That's the way they did things in the olden days, and that's the way the old man and I did them. These are my terms, not his. I don't know if the old man knew the words *master, journeyman,* and *apprentice.* I don't know if his English was good enough to know those sorts of words.

I observed him. I used to watch his every move.

Under cover of darkness, the old man and I used to go out. We escaped from Nine Mile Trailer Park and headed out for scavenging night. Possibility was there, waiting for me. An old colander with only one of its three little curved metal legs was there. You would think that someone had known I was coming, and left it there, bagless, unboxed, so that I would be sure to see it. It was the kind of colander that they still make, that they have been making for all eternity—a round metal bowl with holes in the shape of stars punched all through it, propped on three little curved metal legs that are screwed into the bottom.

Two of the legs were missing, and the colander was tilted. It was a lame and punch-drunk colander.

I held it up to my face and pushed my nose up against the bottom of the bowl. My face was encased in colander. It smelled cold and clean, like clean metal. Someone must have washed it before they put it out for the trash. Maybe they debated before they put it into the trash. Maybe they thought, there's got to be more use in this colander. Maybe they tried to make little legs for it to stand on, so that they could continue to use the star-shaped-hole colander. It might have been a going-away gift from the owner's mother, or a wedding gift from fifty years before. But because the owner of this colander did not understand the art of metalworking, they were unable to fix the colander.

"A new colander is only a few bucks at the hardware store," you can imagine someone saying to them. "Get rid of this old thing."

I looked at the old man. He nodded. That's how I knew I was learning, learning to see with the old man's eyes.

The colander owner did not have the old man's eyes. The colander owner could not see the art of possibility, the possibility of beauty. They did not have the hands and the tools to repair the snapped-off legs of the colander and make it whole again, make it new again, so that it would stand upright and fulfill its potential.

Sometimes we stopped at Crystal's Diner. I had a milkshake. He had a cup of coffee.

He left things at the diner. The money for the milkshake and coffee, plus a quarter. Always that. But he left other things too, things that he made, things that we made together. Sugar cookies wrapped in a tinfoil swan for Crystal. Once a bracelet made of curled-up soda pop tops strung on a piece of red string. The kind of thing that Crystal's nephew Johnny is crazy for. Shinies, and small red things, that's what Johnny loves.

On our way out once, as we passed Johnny's booth, I saw the old man's hand go into his pocket and come out again. The candelier cookie cutter lay shining up from Johnny's table. Johnny wasn't there, but it waited for him. Next week when we went back to the diner, there was Johnny, waving the candelier in the air under the light, so that it threw sparkles onto the chrome sugar shaker.

The old man knew things about people.

On our first trip under cover of darkness, with me as his apprentice, we walked by Mrs. J'Alexander's house. Her son was sitting in the window. He can't talk. He can't walk. That happened in the Vietnam War.

"Her son almost died," I told him. "His name's Joe. His legs were blown off in the war."

Everyone knows that. It's common knowledge.

"He's deaf dumb and blind," I said.

"He is not," the old man said.

"It's common knowledge," I said.

"Knowledge is not common."

"He can't hear, he can't talk, and he can't see," I said. "That makes you deaf dumb and blind."

"He can see and he can hear."

I looked in the window, lit up by a lamp. Joe was sitting in his wheelchair.

"What can he see? What can he hear?"

"Everything you can."

If that's true, how did the old man know it?

"Are you psychic?" I said.

He shook his head. It could be that the old man didn't know that word, or it could be that he was truly not psychic. Then I remembered that I was an apprentice and I stopped talking. I made a vow to continue to observe the old man and learn his ways.

I didn't know then that our time was almost up.

I am still the old man's apprentice in all things. Paul Revere started that way. Back in those days there was a system for apprentices and journeymen and masters. You followed in their footsteps. That's how Paul Revere learned to mold silver and create useful objects of great beauty. I've seen the Revere-ware factory in Rome. It's only fifteen miles away. I've been past it at night, when the red neon horse gallops against the dark sky. I think about that horse sometimes. I think about the young Paul Revere, apprentice to a master craftsman.

# Chapter Thirteen

Once, when I was still eleven and the old man was still alive although I had not yet met him, I asked Tamar a sraightforward, answer-demanding question.

"Ma, did you want kids?"

Tamar looked at me. I looked back at her. I raised my eyebrows and held them up there.

"Yes."

That was it. That was her answer. No quibbling, no equivocating, no hemming or hawing. It took me by surprise.

"You did?"

"Yes. I did."

That gave me something to chew on. As my hermit grandfather chewed on deerskin through the long winter to make it soft and pliable and ready for the needle, so did I chew on Tamar's answer. She was busy with her lumberjacket. How she loves her lumberjacket. Her mother bought it at the store in Speculator. I used to think eighteen was old enough so that your mother could die, but now I'm not sure.

Tamar was working the new zipper on her lumberjacket, trying to get the teeth to fit together smoothly and not snaggle halfway up. She had replaced the zipper herself when it gave out. Tamar is not a seamstress, however. Neither a needler nor a threader shall she be. Already the zipper had come apart at the bottom. Tamar was using duct tape to keep it together. When the duct tape made its appearance, I asked another answer-demanding question.

"Did you fall in love with him?" I said to Tamar.

She didn't look up. She was wrapping the duct tape around the bottom of the broken zipper.

"Were you in love with my father?" I said. "Even for just that one time?"

Duct tape doesn't tear. You have to cut it. She cut it with the kitchen shears, as opposed to the tiny sharp scissors on her Swiss army knife, which would have gummed up had she tried to use them on duct tape. Tamar can't stand her Swiss army scissors to be gummed.

"Even for a few minutes? I'm just trying to understand."

"No," Tamar said. "I did not love your father."

"At all?"

"At all."

"Then why did you do that with him?"

"Well, that will have to remain a mystery," Tamar said.

She finished wrapping the zipper and smoothed down the duct tape seam. Then she slipped her feet into her worn-out moccasins and wiggled her toes. I watched her face for a silent wince. That happens sometimes, when her toes are remembering being frozen. There was nothing.

"Why?"

"Because."

"Things don't have to remain mysteries."

"This one does," Tamar said. "There are some things you are too young to understand."

That was a rare thing for Tamar to say. Usually she stops after, "This one does," and that would be the end of it. Tamar is not a qualifier of words. Things are, things are not. That's the sort of person she is.

"I'm not a child," I said.

But that was it. She was finished. She stretched her arms in her old lumberjacket carefully, so that the worn-out seams wouldn't rip any farther, and tested the zipper for snags.

"There's going to come a point at which you will be forced to buy a new lumberjacket," I said. "There will come a day when you will get in the car and drive to Speculator, walk into the lumberjacket store, and buy a new one."

But even now, that day has not yet come. That day in Speculator remains in the future. There's no way to predict when it will come, no way to know when Tamar will wake, put on the lumberjacket her mother gave her, look down at it and realize that it is no more, that the seams are destroyed and it will not zip. That the cold cannot be kept out. The lumberjacket as it once was will have disappeared. Tamar's lumberjacket from her mother will have entered a new, nonjacket life, and in her gut Tamar will know it.

When you lose your hair in a fire, you might not recognize it when it grows back in. It doesn't look like the same hair that grew on your head your whole life long. New hair is soft, and patchy. When new hair grows in over a patch of scalp that was burned in a fire, it grows in tentatively, unsure it should be there. You look at your hair in the mirror and you wonder whose hair it is, and if it's always been this way and you just never noticed it before.

Think about it. You walk around with dead hair hanging off your head. The only thing about hair that's alive is its roots. The roots push up new hair, but that new hair is already dead. In a way, having your hair burned off in a fire is not a tragedy at all; that hair was not alive.

They hauled the old man's trailer away. One day it was there, with bent metal strips hanging out of the black windows, with black cement steps leading up to the door that was burned away, with the curved kitchen end burnt into a lump, and then the next day it wasn't.

"Where's Georg's trailer?" I asked Tamar.

I've started calling him *Georg*, so that anyone who's listening will know the way his name was pronounced.

"They hauled it away."

"To where?"

"I'm not sure."

"Who hauled it?"

"I don't know."

"Then how do you know it was hauled?"

"That's what they do with trailers that are too old, or burnt up, or are otherwise unusable."

Did anyone go through the old man's trailer before they hauled it away? Did anyone search through the rubble to see if there was anything worthwhile preserving in the ruins? Were there people with masks and white suits and boots, moving slowly from miniature room to miniature room, sifting through the ashes, looking for remnants of the old man's life?

"Did they take the forge, too?" I asked Tamar.

"What forge?"

"His forge," I said. "Don't you even know about his *forge*?"

"No."

"He was a metalworker," I said. "Have you ever heard of a metalworker without a forge?"

"No," Tamar said. "I guess I haven't."

"Have you ever heard of a metalworker without tin snips? Jewelry pliers? A soldering iron? A torch? Pre—cookie cutters?"

"Pre—cookie cutters," Tamar said. "Pre, cookie, cutters."

"That's right," I said. "Pre—cookie cutters. Don't ask me to explain. Don't ask me to show you the relationship between things. Don't ask me about consistencies, and objects that are beautiful as well as useful."

Tamar looked at me. Words kept spilling out of me, secret words, words and phrases that were the old man's and mine. I ran out of the room to stop those precious words from wasting themselves in the blank air between Tamar and me.

I asked Mr. Jewell if he knew what had happened to the forge.

"I don't know, Miss Clara," he said. "One day the trailer was there, and the next it wasn't, and I don't know what happened to the forge."

No one knew. I wondered about the forge. Did someone under cover of darkness steal into the ruins and take it while I was in the hospital with burned lungs? Is someone in North Sterns now working with fire at a backyard forge? Or did it tumble into Nine Mile Creek when the fire trucks were putting out the fire? Is it possible that the forge is even now rusting in the dark water of Nine Mile Creek? In the fullness of time the destiny of the old man's forge may be revealed to me. But I doubt it.

The old man had no family. He had no friends, except silent friends. His silent friends were friends like Crystal Zielinski at Crystal's Diner, who took the onions that the old man brought her and chopped them into tuna salad. Friends like Harold Jewell, who sometimes used to give the old man a Persian doughnut for free.

"He has the money to pay for that Persian," I said to Mr. Jewell once.

I wanted Mr. Jewell to know that the old man was not a bag person. He had a home and an onion garden. He had a visitor every Wednesday night. He had enough money to pay for a Persian doughnut without it being given to him for free.

"You don't have to feel sorry for the old man," I said to Mr. Jewell.

He gave me a look.

"I don't feel sorry for Mr. Kominsky, Clara," Mr. Jewell said. "I give him a Persian doughnut because I consider him my friend."

*I am the last of my line,* the old man had said to me in the beginning of my oral history project. That was one of the first things the old man ever said to me, despite the fact that he was chary with his words.

"Did the fire start because the old man used a can of flammable stuff in the wrong way?" I said. "Is that how it started?"

Tamar looked at me.

"What are you really asking?" she said.

If it had been common knowledge in Sterns that the old man didn't know how to read, then Tamar would have immediately known what I was trying to ask. What I was trying to ask was: if the old man had known how to read, would the fire not have started? Would the old man still be alive? Would

I still be going down on Wednesday nights while Tamar was at choir practice, eating toast thickly spread with margarine and drinking hot chocolate with extra milk?

"Did he use something flammable in the wrong way? Did he not pay attention to the directions?"

She was still looking at me.

"Are you what-iffing?" she said. "Are you retracing? Are you saying if that hadn't happened then that wouldn't have happened and that wouldn't have happened and the old man would still be alive?"

I looked back at her.

"Is that what you're doing?" she said.

"What I'm doing," I said, "is asking if the old man neglected to read the fine print."

"What does it matter, Clara?" Tamar said. "What does it matter now?"

Tamar forgot about my chickens when I was in the hospital. For three weeks in March, a flock of insane chickens were without food or water. Insane chickens paced and pecked the cracked concrete floor of the broken-down barn, while Tamar slept on a cot by the side of my bed at Utica Memorial. The day I got home I put on my boots and headed down there. Tamar was busy patching her moccasins with duct tape.

I walked into the broken-down barn, breathing through my mouth because of the stink of the chicken manure. It was quiet. No peeps, no clucks. No pecking and scratching around in the dirt. I put my sneakers one in front of the other like an Indian guide. I glided up to the pen, stuck my head over the side.

All their necks were broken. I could tell by the weird angles of their heads. My chickens had died not by starvation but by murder. Over in the corner the dollhouse lay tipped on its side, with a chicken lying half-in and half-out of the living room, its wing sticking through the window. Over in the other corner there was a hole burrowed through the broken-down barn siding. Weasel, I thought. I knew about weasels from my research. They kill for fun, just to be mean. They might suck a little blood, but that's it.

Tamar put on her boots right away when I told her the chickens were all dead.

"Oh Jesus," she said. "I completely forgot about them."

"They died not from starvation but from murder," I said. "A weasel got them while I was in the hospital."

She wasn't listening. "I can't believe it," she said. "They never once crossed my mind. Clara, I am so sorry."

But halfway across the pasture Tamar stopped and got a look on her face.

"Clara, what is that smell?"

I tried to pretend I didn't know what she was talking about.

"Smell?" I said. "What smell?"

Then I saw the way Tamar was looking at me.

"Oh, that smell," I said. "I guess I do smell it after all. Dead chickens."

"That isn't dead chickens I'm smelling, Clara."

She started walking fast toward the broken-down door to the broken-down barn.

"Ma," I called.

The back of her ripped lumberjacket was getting away from me.

"What," she called back without turning around.

"Ma! I forgot to tell you that those chickens were not normal. They were abnormal chickens. They were . . . *psychotic* chickens."

She turned around.

"Yes," I said. "Psychotic chickens. The rooster tried to kill me."

I scrabbled around on my scalp where there was still hair, searching for old scabs to show her. Too late, though. She was already into the barn.

"My God," she said.

I came up behind her. Afraid to touch her plaid shoulder. I looked around the barn with her eyes. Fermenting feed in heaps in the pen, where the water I tossed had landed on the feed I spilled. Piles of chicken manure smeared on the pitted cement floor. Massacred chickens strewn like garbage. A searing smell of sulphur and manure and death. Tamar's eyes turned on me were full of a look I had never seen from her before.

"You smell that sulphur smell, Clara? On top of the manure smell?"

"Yes."

"Well, there's a pile of eggs somewhere in this pen. Those hens were laying all this time."

Tamar opened up the gate and walked on in. She waded through the smeary manure piles, kicked a dead hen out of the way. She went over to the pile of hay in the corner and swiped off the top wisps.

"Here they are."

There they were. A million brown eggs, a mountain of brown eggs. Some crushed against each other, some whole and perfect. I stared at that pile of eggs. There was a little heave from the heap of dark feathers in the dollhouse. Another little heave. It was the CJ Wilson chicken. I crouched down in front of him. His beady eye stared back. He kicked a yellow claw. I could tell he was not going to live. I didn't know how he had managed to live as long as he had.

I started to sing to him. "Oh Susannah, oh don't you cry for me . . . For I've come from Alabama, with my banjo on my knee."

I couldn't remember the rest of the words.

"Clara," Tamar said.

She came up and knelt by me and the CJ Wilson chicken. She put her arms around me.

"Why didn't you tell me?" she said.

"Tell you what?"

"Tell me about these chickens."

"What about them?"

Tamar squeezed my arms and rocked. "Everything about them," she said.

"There's not much to tell," I said. "They're not normal chickens. They never were. They're psychotic chickens, especially that CJ Wilson one."

Tamar's arms around me were too tight.

"Could you stop?" I said. "I can't breathe."

All around us the smell rose, thick and heavy. I felt as if I were choking to death in a broken-down barn full of dead insane chickens. All the months, the months and months I had kept the secret of my vicious chickens came crowding down on me and I couldn't stand it. Days and weeks and months of not telling anyone about the chickens, their meanness and cruelty, the way they kept after me, pecking and hissing and clawing, came crawling up out of the heaps of dead dark feathers, snaking around me, invisible and strangling. I started to cry and I couldn't stop.

"You should have told me," Tamar said. "You should have told me about these chickens."

"Why?" I said.

"I could have helped."

"You wouldn't have helped. You've never helped."

Words, crawling out of me, me not stopping them. Tamar's arms falling away and a choking sound coming from her. The smell of death rising around us like the locusts that once ate up all of Laura Ingalls Wilder's summer fields, and the CJ Wilson chicken convulsing where he lay. Tamar leaned away from me.

"You never told me about my grandfather, or my father, or Baby Girl," I said. "No matter how many times I asked, you never told me. That's the only thing I have ever asked you for help with, and you never helped."

Tamar reached out to the CJ Wilson chicken but didn't touch it. She took a deep breath of the rotten air around us.

"You listen to me," she said. "Listen to me, Clara Winter."

I held my breath against the stench of the broken-down barn and listened.

"There is nothing I could tell you that would help," Tamar said.

I kept holding my breath.

"Nothing would help, and everything would hurt," Tamar said.

I stared at CJ, lying there, heaving up now and then, its black eye dull. You must kill this chicken, I told myself. I said it out loud to give myself strength. *You must put him out of his misery.*

"Don't worry," I said to the chicken. I bent down close to where its ear must be. "Don't you worry. It won't hurt."

Quick and clean, I thought. Make it quick and clean.

I picked up a chunk of broken-off cement and I brought it down on CJ Wilson's head.

# Chapter   Fourteen

T amar was at the kitchen sink brushing her teeth when
  C. Winter came to the door. I recognized him immediately. He was the same man who had sat in his apartment on
Genesee Street in Utica, unable to meet my gaze. He came up
the steps to the kitchen door. Tamar was behind me. One of
her many oddities is that she prefers to brush her teeth at the
kitchen sink, in front of the window. She likes the morning
light, she says. At night, when it's dark, she brushes in the
bathroom.

"Hey," he said.

What do you say to your grandfather, when you don't
know him?

"Hi."

Behind me the sound of brushing stopped. I felt Tamar
walking across the kitchen. The air she displaced moved
before her. She held her toothbrush like a gun.

"Tamar?" my biological grandfather said.

She said nothing. She stood there with toothpaste foaming
out of her mouth. When Tamar brushes her teeth she brushes
for a long time. She leans against the sink and stares out the

window while she brushes. I timed her once: five minutes, thirty-three seconds.

"Tamar," he said again.

He took his hat off. It was a Yankees baseball cap, one with the intertwined N and Y. That's what they used to do in the olden days. A gentlemen, in the presence of a lady, would take his hat off. It was a social given. It would have been an extreme insult not to take your hat off in the presence of a lady. There were other places you had to take your hat off, too. Church, indoors, dinner. That was the social *more* of the time.

Tamar said nothing. She stood there with her toothbrush. She looked at him.

"Hi," I said again to C. Winter.

"Hi," he said.

C. Winter still couldn't look at me. His eyes kept moving around. He stood there with his baseball cap in his hands. The time for hesitation was past. She who hesitates is lost, and much had already been lost. I looked up at C. Winter and asked him a question.

"Why did you take Glass Factory instead of Route 12?"

He twirled the cap in his hands. His eyes darted. He said nothing.

"Route 12 would've been plowed," I said. "What was your reasoning?"

He shrugged.

"Please," I said. "Tell me."

He looked up at me. Tamar stood still beside me. The toothpaste on her brush was drying. I could see it turning hard and white. My biological grandfather cleared his throat.

"Tamar—" he said.

"Please," I said. "Please."

"Because I made a mistake," C. Winter said.

I felt around for my roll of note-taking adding-machine paper in its useful and beautiful paper holder, but it was gone. It was lost to flames, and unlike the famous Rocky Mountain lodgepole pine it would never regenerate. I resorted to air-writing. *Because I made a mistake,* I wrote in the air with my nose. Clifford Winter gave me a look but I kept on.

"You made a lot of mistakes," Tamar said. The white foam at the sides of her mouth was dry, too. It moved along with her jaw when she talked.

"Tamar—"

"*Dad.*"

"I did," C. Winter said.

"Grampa?" I said.

They both turned to me. *Grampa* was a surprise word, an ambush word, startling them both, hanging in the air like a bubble.

"What was my father's name?" I said.

He might come out with it. My father's name might be waiting on the tip of C. Winter's tongue, and topple off, and then I could write it in the air with my nose. I could write it and keep it forever. For the rest of my days, my father's name would be mine, to have and to hold. C. Winter said nothing.

"My father's name," I said. "What was it?"

Nothing.

"Her father's name," Tamar said. "What was it?"

He shook his head.

"Surprise surprise," Tamar said. "I don't know it either."

"I'm talking to my grandfather," I said.

"So am I," she said.

"But you can't *remember* his name," I said.

"I never *knew* his name. There's a difference."

C. Winter reached over and put his cap onto the stack of wood in the woodbin. He placed it carefully on the top row of wood, which I myself had stacked. I take pleasure in stacking wood. Even in a woodbin, which is meant to hold chunks of wood any which way, I will stack. I like neat and orderly stacks of wood.

"You did so know his name," I said. "You just forgot it, is what you said."

"I never knew it," Tamar said.

C. Winter rocked back and forth on the balls of his feet. Tamar threw her toothbrush, with its stiffened bristles, at his cap. It hit the intertwined NY and didn't leave a mark. I wrote Tamar's words in the air: *never knew his name.*

"So neither of you know my father's name," I said. "And you made a mistake in taking Glass Factory."

"Yes," my grandfather said.

"Did you have any knowledge of infant CPR?"

He looked up at me.

"What's that?"

"Infant cardiopulmonary resuscitation. Did you have any knowledge of it?"

He shook his head. Still rocking.

"Did you try to save my sister?" I said.

Rocking.

"Was there any attempt made on the part of either of you to save my baby sister?"

I looked at Tamar, who was looking at C. Winter, who was looking at the porch floor.

"My father's name is unknown," I said. "You by mistake took Glass Factory Road. Neither of you knew infant CPR, nor did you try to save my baby sister. Is that right?"

No answer.

"Is that right?"

No answer.

"And what about winter?" I said. "What about the ice and the snow? What about trucks in ditches?"

"They didn't have infant CPR back then," Tamar said.

"It was eleven years ago," I said. "Of course they did."

"Eleven years ago is a lifetime to you," Tamar said. "But all it is is a snap of the fingers."

She snapped her fingers, something she's very good at. There was a crack on the porch like a whip; that's how good she is at snapping.

"They didn't think about things like that back then," Tamar said.

"You tried, though."

That was C. Winter. He was still rocking. His head was still shaking. Back and forth it swung.

"You tried, Tamar."

I looked at him.

"Your mother tried to save your sister," he said.

I fell. You can fall while sitting down, strapped into a bungee cord safety system in your car, and you can fall from a standing position. I fell on the porch and then I wrapped my arms around my knees. His words went scrolling along the bottom of my mind: *your sister, your sister, your sister.*

"So I had one," I said. "I had a sister."

"Yes, you had a sister."

"No," Tamar said. "Sisters are alive. Sisters are living. Clara never had a sister."

"She did," my grandfather said. "She had a sister."

I closed my eyes and watched the words in my head: *sister, sister, sister.* I had had a baby sister. We had swum together, drunk the same salty water, heard the same sounds. From far away Tamar's voice had come to us over months. We had known the sound of her voice, and the way she moved. We had known the rhythm and feel of our mother's heartbeat as she lay sleeping in darkness that for us remained dark. My sister might have held my hand. She might have touched my face. If babies can love before they're in this world, my sister might have loved me.

"What was her name?" I said.

"Her name was Daphne," my grandfather said.

*Her name was Daphne.* My grandfather moved across the porch. He stretched out his hand to Tamar.

"Tamar."

Tamar was crying.

"She had no name," she said.

"You gave her a name," my grandfather said. "Her name was Daphne. Daphne Winter."

"She never had a chance."

"No, she didn't," my grandfather said.

Then his arm went around Tamar. She didn't hug him. She didn't lean her head on his shoulder. She just stood there, crying. She didn't wipe the tears off her cheeks, or blow her dripping nose. She just stood there.

"I'm sorry," my grandfather said.

"Sorry's not good enough," she said.

He rocked on his heels and kept on rocking and finally Tamar turned around and went inside. I was alone on the porch with C. Winter.

"What are you sorry about?" I asked.

"You name it, I'm sorry about it."

"Are you sorry that you took Glass Factory?"

"Yes."

"Are you sorry about Daphne?"

"Yes."

"Are you sorry about Clara winter?"

He looked at me. I didn't know I was going to say that until I heard it coming out of my mouth. *Are you sorry about Clara winter?* I could hear the words hanging between us.

"Yes," he said. "I'm sorry about Clara winter."

He said it with a lowercase w. I could hear it. I could hear it in his voice, and the way the word formed itself on his tongue: *winter.*

"Would you say your own name for the record?"

"Cliff Winter."

"Clifford Winter," I said.

"That's right."

He said his own name with an ordinary W. But that wasn't what I was thinking. I was thinking how, if I had known my nonhermit grandfather from the time I was a baby, I would know that he was known as Cliff. I wouldn't have to ask him, for the record, what his full name was.

"What else are you sorry about, Mr. Winter?"

He was still on the porch, rocking. He could rock from the balls of his feet to his heels and then roll back up again in a smooth movement. His hands were in his pockets. His baseball cap was still lying on the top row of stacked wood. He nodded over at the wood.

"I'm sorry I didn't see you stack that wood," he said. "That would have been a pretty sight, I'm sure."

"How did you know it was me who stacked it?" I said. "It could have been Tamar."

"No," he said. "Tamar is not a stacker. She's a thrower. When it comes to wood, Tamar's careless."

It was true. Tamar doesn't care about stacking wood. She feels that it's just as good to toss it up on the porch in a jumble and then pluck a piece from the jumble on an as-needed basis. Tamar cares not for neatness in firewood. Were it not for me, we would have a porch strewn with chunks of wood. No rhyme, no reason.

"That's something I'm very sorry to have missed," he said. "Having a granddaughter who's a stacker. Who taught you to stack like that?"

"I taught myself," I said. "I looked through the catalogs and saw how they stacked the firewood in the pictures."

He nodded. "Mmhm," he said. "Just as I suspected."

I laughed. I couldn't help it. Then he started laughing. We both laughed, him rocking, me holding onto the post by the steps.

"But I'll tell you what I'm most sorry about," he said when we were finished laughing. "Clara winter. That's what I'm most sorry about."

The old man as a young man might have stood across the street and stared at a young girl named Juliet, and loved her.

Someday, maybe, I will be walking into Jewell's Grocery, or standing on a folding chair in the Twin Churches church-house, and a boy will look at me and love me. It's possible. It could happen.

It doesn't always happen that way though.

Take Tamar. She did not love my father, nor did he love her. She does not know his name, and it's doubtful if he ever knew hers. She wasn't lying. She was telling the truth.

The music was extremely loud, is what Tamar told me. The music was so loud that no one could hear her.

"He turned up the music," she said.

For a while that's all she said. She put her hands over her ears as if she was hearing the loud music. Tamar hates loud music. She will not allow loud music in the house. When Tamar listens to music she listens to the radio at a volume so low that I can barely hear it. She does not wake up to music, nor does she like to listen to it at a volume above a whisper. When I set my clock radio, I do not set it to music. I set it to WIBX's morning radio show, which is conversation, and I set it at a whisper. This I do in respect for Tamar.

I didn't know what Tamar was telling me.

"He turned up the music?"

She nodded. "Way up. No one could hear me."

"No one heard you."

That's something you can do if you're not sure of what to say to someone else. You can repeat what they say, with a little twist. You can turn a statement into a question, such as "he turned up the music?" or you can twist the statement and repeat it, as in "no one heard you," instead of "no one could hear you."

"No one," she said.

She put her hands over her ears again. She rocked back and forth, like her father had done on the porch when he said he was sorry.

"How old were you?" I said.

"Eighteen."

I thought about that for a while. Eighteen is how old Tamar was when her mother died. I used to think that eighteen was not a young age. It was almost twenty, and twenty used to seem quite old.

"My mother had just died," Tamar said as if she could read my thoughts. "It took a long time for her to die. I ran away. I couldn't stand it, stuck in the house with my father and that incessant sadness."

Incessant is not a word I would have associated with Tamar. Even as she spoke and I listened, the word *incessant* went scrolling across the bottom of my mind.

"All I could see ahead of me was days and nights and weeks and years of sadness and quiet and darkness and stale air in a shut-up house," Tamar said. "I was too young. I couldn't see that a day would come when it would get better."

"Where did you want to go?" I said.

"Florida."

"Why Florida?"

"Sun. Beach. No more winter."

"But you love winter," I said. "You're Tamar, lover of snow and cold and ice."

She shook her head. "It was a long time ago," she said. "A long, long time ago."

"Not so long ago," I said. "Twelve years, is all."

"Twelve years and a lifetime."

"So what happened?" I said.

"What happened is what I told you. I packed my bag. I left. I went to a party at Roy Cover's house because his house was in Utica and the Greyhound station was three blocks away and the bus left at 2:00 A.M. And when it was time to go I went upstairs to get my sweatshirt—you don't need a winter jacket in Florida—and he followed me and shut the door and locked the door and turned the music up."

"Roy Cover?"

"No. Not Roy Cover. Him. The guy."

The guy.

"My father?"

Tamar barked. That's what you call that kind of a laugh. "You don't have a father," she said.

"Did my grandfather know what happened at the party?" I said to Tamar.

"Yes. Your grandfather knew."

"So what happened then?"

"What happened was that your grandfather told me it was my own fault, and that he would not help me raise the child. You're on your own, Tamar, is what he said."

*You're on your own, Tamar. That's all she wrote. End of story. No ifs ands or buts. Sore subject. Moving right along.*

The next time C. Winter came to the house on a secret Wednesday night visit I asked him about it. Usually he sat on the porch and talked to me while Tamar was at choir practice.

"Did you know what happened to Tamar at that party in Utica?" I asked him.

"Yes."

"Did you tell her it was her fault?"

"Yes."

We sat there for a while. It was cold.

"On my next birthday I'll be thirteen," I said.

"I know."

"Why didn't you ever come out here before?"

"I did, once, a few months after it happened."

"And?"

"And I saw Tamar out by the barn splitting wood. You were in the house bawling. I saw that I hadn't split enough wood for half a winter's worth, and she was out there chopping away, and you were screaming, and I thought of what happened to Daphne, and I turned around and left."

"And that's when you went up north to live in the primeval forest?"

He looked at me. "What?"

"Tamar told me you lived in a tipi in a small primeval forest up near the Vermont border."

"She did?"

Then I remembered that Tamar hadn't told me that. I had made that up. It was a figment of my imagination.

"No, she didn't," I said. "I made it up. It all started with *Tales from the Cave: Story of an Adirondacks Hermit.*"

"I have no idea what you are talking about," C. Winter said. "Anyway. I went back to Utica. I left Tamar chopping and you screaming. And now I'm back and Tamar's at choir practice and you're twelve. And that's the end of the story."

The old man taught me how to see the possibility of beauty. He taught me how to make objects that are useful as well as beautiful. I keep my eyes open. At any moment something may shine out at me. There may be something sparkling in the ditch. It may be half-buried beneath fallen maple leaves. Last fall I went walking down Williams Road, the colors of autumn flaming in the trees. Someone was burning leaves even though it's not allowed anymore.

I smelled those burning leaves and thought, I will never leave. I will never leave the Sterns Valley in the foothills of the Adirondack Mountains, where burning leaves smell this way in the fall.

I lay down in the middle of Williams Road, which is a dirt road where almost no cars ever come, and looked up at the sky. *A September blue sky,* is what Tamar would have said. Her words scroll across the bottom of my mind like all words scroll. I'll never not be able to read. I'll be a prisoner of letters the rest of my life. Every time I sign my name I'll remember the way the old man signed his name, the way he made a slash instead of a dot above the "i," the way he underlined his last name as if someone might not take it the way he intended.

The morning after the CJ Wilson chicken died I woke up and I knew that Georg Kominsky, American Immigrant, was truly gone. I could picture him, sitting on his chair at the cigarette-burned kitchen table where we used to drink our coffee and our hot chocolate. But the table was gone and the kitchen was gone and the forge was gone and the trailer was gone and the old man was gone and so was my roll of green adding-machine paper.

That roll of adding-machine paper contained all my notes for my future true book about Georg Kominsky, American Immigrant. There were words on that spool of paper that were the first words I ever heard the old man speak, and there were words on there that were among his last. Bits of the old man were caught on that paper. I had planned to keep it for the rest of my life, so that I could take it out and unroll it whenever I wanted, and remember the old man.

Will there be more spools of paper in the reject bin at Jewell's? There are no guarantees. It's a reject bin. It's a bin filled with items that others don't want, that don't sell, that have flaws, that are in some way peculiar.

"It takes a certain kind of person to want a roll of green adding-machine paper," Mr. Jewell said when I bought it. "And you, Clara Winter, are that sort of person."

Just before it was lost in the fire, I came to the end of the roll. The notes for *Georg Kominsky: American Immigrant* were finished. All the raw material, the heart and soul of the old man, was there. It's amazing to reach the end of an entire spool of adding-machine paper. When I first bought it, when I had just chosen it from its peers in the bin at Jewell's Grocery, I thought it would last forever. It was a pristine spool of paper. Untouched by human hands. When I wrote my first word on the first inch of narrow, curling green paper, I never stopped to think that one day the spool would be filled. But words turn into sentences turn into paragraphs turn into curl after curl of writing, bouncing on the floor.

The old man as a boy of seventeen must have tried to find help, someone, anyone, a cottage in the woods, to help him carry his young brother Eli to safety. Why couldn't there have been a cottage in the woods, smoke coming out of the chimney, paned windows with firelight glowing behind the glass, visible even in the middle of a blizzard? Inside a family sits around a table covered with a red-checked cloth. A gun hangs over the fireplace mantel. The man of the family is a hunter, wise to the ways of the woods. He comes immediately when Georg pounds on the door. They retrace Georg's steps, fast disappearing in the whiteout conditions, and make their way back to Eli, lying helpless in the snow. Together they make a seat with interlocked hands, the way they taught us to do in gym class at Sterns Elementary, and carry Eli to safety. The wife of the family makes hot broth and spoons it into Eli's mouth. They wrap him in feather quilts and stoke the fire. Winter rages outside the door, winds howl, but inside all is safe and warm. In a few days Eli has recovered enough to start out on the journey again. The snow has stopped and all is peaceful and calm, a winter wonderland of quiet whiteness.

"Bon voyage," the hunter says.

His wife presses a basket of bread and cheese and dried berries into their hands. They wish them well on their journey to America.

"Remember us," the wife says.

I almost wrote that whole story down on my adding-machine roll of paper. Everything was good. Everything worked out. Eli recovered. He did not lose any fingers or toes. Together Eli and Georg made their way to the dock, together they endured the hard Atlantic crossing. They ate hardtack belowdecks and drank musty barreled water from the same tin ladle. Together they entered America through Ellis Island. They lived together forever, as close as only brothers can be.

I almost asked the old man about that cottage once.

"What about the cottage in the woods?" I almost said. "What about the hunter, and the roaring fire, and the featherbed?"

# Chapter Fifteen

The story of my birth is an astounding one. I was born during a February blizzard in a truck tipped sideways into a ditch on Glass Factory Road. My grandfather was trying to get Tamar to Utica Memorial in time for the delivery, but there was no such luck. The most amazing part of the story of my birth is that my mother, Tamar, delivered me herself. There was no one there to help her, including my grandfather, who was trying to slog through a blizzard to reach a house and get help. My mother, Tamar, had to push. She knew that once you have to push there's no going back.

Tamar closed her eyes and prayed to God that the urge to push would stop. She felt darkness closing in on her, and the winds of the blizzard howling around her, and she was afraid. Please God, keep my baby safe, she prayed. She did not know that there were two babies.

Outside, in the depths of the blizzard, my grandfather kept on. Sheer luck kept him from losing his way in the darkness of the night and the whiteness of the snow. He found a house. The people who lived there called the police. But there was nothing that could be done. The blizzard was that bad. Even had it been on Route 12, the police said, there was no way an emergency vehicle could get through in that kind of weather. My grandfather headed back to the truck. He tried to retrace his steps but his steps were gone. By the grace of God he found the truck but it was hours later and hours too late. Tamar was unconscious and Daphne was dead. I was alive, lying on Tamar's bare stomach, covered with her parka.

"And that's the story," Tamar said.

"That's the whole story," my grandfather said.

"That's not the story I made up," I said. "My story had a midwife in it, named Angelica Rose Beaudoin."

Tamar and my grandfather said nothing. We were sitting on the porch. Piles of wood left over from the winter, neatly stacked, stood silent around us. It was a cloudless night in the Adirondacks. High in the firmament, stars glittered. The air was still and cold and smelled not of spring but of winter, tired old winter whose time was past.

The day after the judge sentenced CJ's father was warm and sunny. I could sense the presence of spring. Underneath the last of the snow, bulbs were beginning to push their way toward light.

"Wipe," CJ said when I got on the bus. His eyes were filled with his hatred for me.

"Guess what," CJ said to the boys. "Me and my dad, we're leaving here. Getting out of this dump. My dad's going back on the road again. Going on a Chucky Luck comeback tour and taking me with him."

CJ was telling the boys about the hotels he was going to stay at and the cars he was going to drive when Tiny pulled up at CJ's trailer.

"Hey CJ!" one of the boys said. "What happened to your famous car? You decide to start a junkyard instead?"

The white Camaro was bashed in on the driver's side. CJ gave the boys the finger. I saw him look over at me.

"Some drunk smashed it up," said CJ. "Some drunk totaled it."

"Some drunk, huh?" said one of the boys. "Go tell that to Chucky Luck."

CJ's ears turned red below his buzzcut. "I *said* a drunk smashed it up."

"Uh huh," said the same boy. "Uh huh."

She who hesitates is lost. I put my hand in my pocket. I was wearing old white Carter's that had a rip at the side seam. I felt for the rip through the thin cotton. Then I leaned out of my seat.

"CJ's right," I said. "He's right. I heard my mother talking about it after court last night. This drunk guy, he just drove right over the yellow line on Glass Factory Road and smashed up CJ's Camaro."

CJ didn't look at me.

"See? I told you," he said to the boys. "That Camaro was rusted-out anyway. It was a mess. I hated it. My dad, he's going to get me a new one instead. A brand-new one, when he starts making money on the tour."

I slid back in my seat and looked out the window at the mountains coming closer. I kept my hand in my pocket, covering up the rip in my Carter's. That was before the state took CJ away and Tiny stopped pulling up at his trailer.

• • •

The old man was a highly prized tinsmith in his former village. Once I asked him about it. You had to space questions few and far between with the old man. He was like Tamar in that way.

"If you were only seventeen when you left your village," I asked the old man, "how could you be such a good tinsmith?"

He didn't answer right away. I didn't have a sense of unanswering, though. I waited.

"It was a different time," the old man said. "It was a different country. People grew up faster. I had been a metalworker for a long time by the time I was seventeen."

That was all he said. There was much that he left out, much I never found out. How had he come to learn the art of metalworking so early? How had he never learned to read? Did his father say: *You must go to work, Georg, there are too many mouths to feed and I cannot earn enough myself.*

Maybe his mother put him to work helping her in her work as a laundrywoman. She may have been a charwoman. It's possible. She may have had a large wicker basket that she took from cottage to cottage in the old man's village that no longer exists, gathering the weekly wash from each family and taking it down to the river, where she washed it in the cold clear water with brown softsoap she made herself. She may have pounded the clothes on the rocks to get out the stubborn stains, like cabbage-roll-with-tomato stains, ox-plow-dirt stains, muddy-boot stains, dried-sweat stains. She then may have draped the wet clothes over lingonberry bushes by the banks of the river to dry in the sun, while she sat and rested after her work. Her hands may have been large-knuckled and reddened from all the washing and pounding and folding. Georg would have helped her. He would have rinsed the soapy clothes.

*Careful, Georg,* she may have said. *Get every bit of soap out. If you leave the soap in the clothes will be scratchy. If the clothes are scratchy we will lose our laundry business and then how will we eat? Your father does not earn enough from farming to feed us. The land is poor and the potatoes do not grow as they should. Take good care, Georg, and rinse the clothes till the water runs clear.*

That's what she may well have said to her son Georg, the little laundry helper. When baby Eli came along six years later she may have laid him in a basket with a cloth draped over it to keep the sun out, letting him sleep by the bank of the river as she and Georg worked. When Georg's father was done in the potato fields he may have come down to the river to wash himself, to dive into the clear cold water and rinse the grime of the fields from his sweaty skin. Then the whole family— mother, father, Georg, and little Eli—would have walked home, Georg's father helping his mother with the heavy wicker basket full of freshly washed and folded laundry, Georg singing songs to baby Eli. They would have had boiled potatoes and cabbage soup for dinner. They would have bowed their heads and given thanks for their humble fare—

The old man's life still tumbles through my heart and soul. A story starts itself and I watch it unfold. The old man is gone. Who am I to say what may or may not have happened, what the old man's life as a child may or may not have been like?

Next time Tamar went to choir practice I rode into Sterns with her. She dropped me at Crystal's Diner so I could wait there while she practiced. Crystal brought me a vanilla milkshake. She knows they're my favorite. Johnny was coloring in his booth.

"Can I sit with Johnny?" I said to Crystal.

"Why not?" she said.

Johnny seemed happy to see me. He had a coloring book and an eight-pack of crayons that were all red. How did that happen? Did Crystal buy eight packs of assorted crayons and then pick out the reds from each one?

"Here," Crystal said. She set a tunafish sandwich down in front of me. It came with a pickle and chips.

"Do you still use real olive oil in your salad dressing?" I said.

"Indeed I do."

Johnny held one of his red crayons up to the lamp and laughed the way he laughs.

"My grandfather's name is C. Winter," I said. "Most people call him Cliff."

"I know," Crystal said. "I remember your grandfather from when Tamar and I were growing up."

"Did his eyes jiggle around back then?" I said.

"I don't remember his eyes doing that."

"Did he rock back and forth?"

"I don't remember him doing that either."

"Do you know if he told Tamar that certain things were her fault that actually were not her fault?" I said.

"No, I do not," Crystal said.

"Do you remember if C. Winter loved Tamar?"

"He must have."

"It's not a law of nature," I said. "It's not written in stone."

"Her mother loved her. Of that I'm sure."

"Her mother died," I said. "So did Georg Kominsky, American Immigrant."

"Yes, he did."

"I don't know C. Winter, and Tamar didn't know Georg Kominsky," I said.

"She knew more about Mr. Kominsky than you might think," Crystal said. "She went to see him. She wrote him a letter about you."

"She did not."

"Yes she did. Before you ever met him. When you told her you were going to do your, what was it, oral history project on him."

A customer came in and sat down on the one of the red stools that twirl around at the counter. Crystal went over to him and took his order. She did not write it down. Crystal has the ability to remember any order given to her, no matter how many people in the group, and she never fails to remember who ordered what. It's one of her talents. After she brought the man his grilled cheese she started wiping down the other end of the counter. I slid out of the booth and went over to where she was scrubbing at a dried chocolate fudge stain with her red rag. All Crystal's rags are red, because of Johnny and his craving for it.

"Why?" I said.

Crystal rinsed the rag and resoaped it and started in on the stool tops. It's not everyone who will scrub the top of every single diner stool every single day.

"Why do you think?" Crystal said. "She was making sure he was all right. She was making sure he was a good person who wouldn't hurt her daughter. She was being a mother."

"She didn't tell me."

"No, she didn't. She thought you wouldn't have wanted her to. Was she right?"

I considered.

"Yes," I said. "Yes, she was right."

Crystal didn't know the old man couldn't read, just as Tamar didn't know. The old man would have taken the letter and nodded his head. I could see him nodding his head, the way he used to do. He might have laid the letter on his kitchen table and let it sit there a while. Then he may well have put the letter into one of his kitchen drawers, ne'er to be touched by human hands, ne'er to be seen by human eyes.

Tamar picked me up at the diner after choir practice. I was helping Johnny write his name. I put my fingers over his and guided his hand around the piece of newspaper we were practicing on. J, o, h, n, n, y. It's not easy to guide someone else's hand in writing. Johnny loved it though. He loved seeing the red crayon letters of his name appear. He laughed and laughed. Tamar ruffled his hair on the way out of the diner.

"Bye, Johnny," she said.

On the way home I pressed my nose against the cold car window. By cupping my hands around my eyes I blocked out the light from the car and stared out at the dark night sky.

"'Tis a clear night," I said to Tamar. "And the stars glitter thickly in the firmament."

"My thoughts exactly," Tamar said. "You took the words right out of my mouth. 'And the stars glitter thickly in the firmament' was right on the tip of my tongue."

"What did you say to the old man when you went to see him before my oral history project?" I said.

An ambush sentence, hanging in the air between us. She didn't miss a beat.

"I told him that you were my daughter, a child of eleven, and that I would kill anyone who harmed you," Tamar said. "I told him I would be watching him."

No hemming or hawing, no mumbling, no prevaricating. That's Tamar.

"And what did he say?"

"He listened. He nodded. He looked at me and I looked at him. We shook hands. I left."

"And what did you say in the letter you wrote to him?"

"I told him about you."

"What about me?"

"I told him that you were a strange child, that he should expect the unexpected when dealing with you. I told him that you were obsessed with the memory of a baby. I told him about your love of books, your book reports, and your stories."

"Stories? What about stories?"

"I told him that stories are the way you look at the world. That stories are your salvation."

*Stories are your salvation.*

"And?" I said.

"And what?"

*And what,* I thought. And what about Daphne Winter? What about a fake Adirondack hermit living in a primeval patch of forest? And what about the old man? What about his trailer, and his forge in the backyard, his dark-green sink in the bathroom? What about his refrigerator that held one quart of milk per week, no more no less, and his cupboard with its three orange-rimmed plates? What about his kitchen drawer that contained letters he couldn't read, the wall lined with hooks that held our cookie cutters? What about the tin paper holder he made for me, and the adding-machine paper that contained his heart and soul?

"What about his heart and soul?" I said to Tamar.

"His heart and soul," she said. "His heart and soul are up to you, Clara. They're your department."

My mother, Tamar, holds contradictions within herself. They coexist, battling each other inside her. She craves and hates her father, C. Winter. She longs for and tries to forget her mother, that slow-dying mysterious woman. There may be no one she loves more than me, but every time she looks at me she sees my sister, Daphne. Warring ghosts fight each other inside my mother's heart, and the battles have made her stern and strong.

# Chapter Sixteen

They never sifted through the ashes of the old man's trailer. I asked the Floyd Volunteer Fire Marshal.

"Did anyone sift through the ashes?" I said. "Did anyone comb through the rubble, looking for anything salvageable from the old man's belongings?"

He shook his head.

"There was nothing left to look through," he said. "It burned to the ground."

"No half-burnt belongings, even?"

"Nothing," he said. "I'm sorry, Clara. I know he was a friend of yours."

If someone had looked, they might have found salvageable objects from the old man's trailer. Things that were scorched, bent from the heat, but still usable. There might have been things that to the untrained eye looked like junk, burnt beyond any conceivable use, but that to the someone in the know would have been useful. The trained eye can see the possibility of beauty and usefulness. The old man, had he not died in the fire at his trailer, had he come across the burnt ruins of another trailer in another time and place, would have sifted through the rubble. The old man would have come away from the ruins of that fire with his hands full of possibility. After a time, the old man would have changed something that was only a possibility into something that existed, something whole, something with a place in the world.

I think about his hands sometimes. The hands of a metalworker are hands that work with fire. Most people may have looked at the old man's hands and seen nothing but fingers, tendon, bone, and the skin that covers them all. They would not have known about the knowledge in the old man's hands, what he knew how to do with his fingers, how he could take something that was a possibility and make it into something real.

If we had had more time, I might have asked him many questions, questions that I did not have time to think of. There are questions waiting in the future, questions that I will come to, and some will be questions that I want to ask the old man, and the old man will not be there to ask.

Some people may have thought of the old man as ugly or evil. The possibility exists that in Sterns, there are people who thought of him in that way. I used to think that the lady two trailers down from the old man thought of him as evil. There was something in the way she used to lean out her window and watch. She never said anything. Sometimes she came out of her door, onto her front step, and watched. If I had to pick, I would have picked that lady as someone who thought of the old man as evil.

But I would have been wrong.

That lady thought highly of the old man. She told me so. When I went back, after I got out of the hospital, and stood by the entrance to where the old man used to live, she came out of her trailer and walked down to where I was standing.

"They hauled it away," she said. "The other day. Put some chains around it, pulled it up onto a flatbed, and then it was gone."

"Where?"

"I don't know," she said.

We stood and looked at where the trailer had been for a while. Then I wanted to go. I had looked enough. There was no rubble to pick through. That had been cleaned up. With what, I don't know.

"Well, bye," I said.

"He was a good man," she said. "He shoveled my steps every snowfall."

"He did?"

"He did. Every snowfall, even an inch or two. An inch or two would've been easy enough to sweep off with my broom, but he was there first."

I turned and started down the dirt road that leads to the entrance. She went back to her trailer.

"I thought very highly of George," she called after me. "He used to bring me onions from his garden."

The possibility of beauty exists in an enameled pot rusted through at the bottom, lying in the woods just off Sterns Valley Road. There's a curved handle on the rusted pot, attached to either side. I lifted it up by the handle and swung it back and forth. It squeaked a little, and the handle was rusty, but the possibility was there.

The old man would have seen it, too.

I have the old man's eyes. He trained me to see the possibility of beauty, and that is what I see. I can see it everywhere, in a dented olive oil can, in an old pioneer pot on the Sterns Valley Road.

Fragments of rusted metal flaked off the worn-out bottom of the pot, and the sides of the pot gave when I pushed on them. It crumpled in my hands, all except for the handle. This pot's been through a fire, I thought. It could have been left over in the ruins of a long-ago blaze on Sterns Valley Road.

This pot may have been a pioneer pot, suspended over the glowing coals of a pioneer fire.

It may have belonged to a pioneer mother on her way west. Every night she used this pot to cook stew for her pioneer husband and children. Every evening her oldest child scrubbed it out with sand by the creek, and every morning the pioneer mother cooked cornmeal mush in it for breakfast. You have to be extremely careful when cooking cornmeal mush. You have to sift the cornmeal into the boiling water in a fine stream between your fingers, stirring constantly all the while, or else the cornmeal mush will be an inedible mess of lumps.

That's a true fact. I read it in a pioneer book.

One morning, as the pioneer family packed up their belongings from camping overnight on what is now the Sterns Valley Road but back then was a nameless trail winding through tall meadow grass, the pioneer mother placed the pot on a pile of quilts near the back of the covered wagon. The quilts were folded neatly after keeping the pioneer family warm through the long cool spring night. The pot rested on top of the patchwork quilts, and the pioneer mother thought it was secure.

"Ready," she called to her pioneer husband, who was up front sitting on the wagon seat with the oldest pioneer child.

"All right then," he called back.

He may not have said "all right then." He may have said something else that meant "all right then." It was a long time ago. It's hard to know exactly.

With a sudden lurch, the covered wagon started moving. The pioneer mother was busy tending to her youngest child, who was a baby still in nappies. That's what they called diapers back then. She did not notice when the cooking pot slipped from its perch atop the patchwork quilts and fell to the ground behind the moving wagon. She did not hear the tiny thump it made as it landed.

That night, the pioneer mother searched frantically for the cookpot. She did not find it. Fifteen miles back, the cookpot lay in the tall grasses. Already, leaves had started to sift over it. A curious primeval woodchuck or skunk sniffed at it, then lost interest and waddled away.

It was their only cookpot. The family went hungry that night and had naught to cook their cornmeal mush in the next morning. The baby, still in nappies, wrapped in a yellow blanket, cried piteously. He wailed mournfully through the night.

What happened to them?

A freak snow fell in Sterns, and the ground was newly white in September. You might think that a September snow in the foothills of the Adirondack Mountains is an impossibility. You would be wrong. On the night of that snowfall, I got out all my false stories. All my books waiting to be written. Waiting for their endings. Waiting to find out what happened.

I stalled for a while. There were more fake book reports than I had thought. They were stacked in a wooden crate that I bought at a garage sale in North Sterns. You wouldn't have thought I'd have had that many ideas for books. If asked I would have said ten, maybe twelve. But there were many more than that. Many, many more, all stacked up. I did not allow myself to go through any of them.

Tamar watched me carry the box out the door. She was eating a jar of marinated artichoke hearts. She likes to eat them with a miniature fork that she says is actually meant for pulling lobster meat out of lobster shells.

Tamar raised her eyebrows.

"Burn barrel," I said. "Cleaning my room. Trash."

It hurt me to say that. It hurt me to call the works of my own imagination trash. I thought of the old man, standing in line on Ellis Island, writing in the air with his nose. I thought of him seeing the official people watching him, talking about him, whispering. I thought of him standing straight and willing them to let him in, him alone, no brother Eli who was supposed to be there, too.

"Trash?" Tamar said. "Are you sure?"

"I'm sure."

"Because they look like book reports to me," Tamar said. "Grade-A book reports, if I'm not mistaken."

"That is correct."

"Read me one," Tamar said.

Read me one. That was something I had never before heard from Tamar, eater of artichoke hearts.

"*Read* you one?"

"Read me one."

I closed my eyes and dug my hand into the box.

"*The Winter Without End,* by Lathrop E. Douglas," I said. "New York: Crabtree Publishers, Inc. 1958."

"Sounds good," Tamar said. "Carry on."

I carried on.

*It was the longest winter that Sarah Martin had ever known. Growing up on the Great Plains, she had known many a stark December, many an endless January, and the bitter winds of February were not unfamiliar to her. She was a child of winter. But that winter—the winter of 1879—Sarah knew true cold.*

*The potatoes had long since run out, as had the cabbages and carrots buried in sand in the root cellar. The meager fire was kept alive with twists of hay. When the first blizzard came, followed every few days by another, Sarah's parents had been trapped in town. It was up to Sarah Martin to keep her baby brother alive and warm until the spring thaw, when her parents could return to the homestead.*

*The true test of Sarah Martin's character comes when her baby brother wanders into the cold in the dead of night. Sarah blames herself for this; she was too busy twisting hay sticks in a corner of the cabin to notice that he had slipped from his pallet next to the fire and squeezed his way outside. "He's only two years old," thinks Sarah. "How long can a tiny child survive outside in this bitter cold?"*

*Will Sarah Martin be able to find her little brother in time? Will she be able to rescue him from a fate so horrible that she cannot bear to think about it?*

*Did Sarah Martin have the foresight to dig a snow tunnel from the house to the pole barn where Bessie and Snowball are stabled? Or is there nothing beyond the cabin door for her beloved brother but blowing snow, bitter wind, and a winter without end?*

*Will Sarah have to face the responsibility of her brother's death?*

*Will her baby brother be forgotten by everyone but her?*

*Will she miss him her whole life long?*
*Read the book and find out.*

Tamar ate the last artichoke heart.

"Well?" she said. "How does it turn out?"

"Read the book and find out."

"It's hard to read a nonexistent book," Tamar said. "You run out of words fast."

How Tamaresque, to have known all along that Clara winter was the author of dozens of nonexistent books. How like Tamar never to have said a word.

"So you tell me," she said. "*Does* Sarah Martin bear the responsibility for her baby brother's death? *Does* everyone forget Sarah Martin's baby brother? *Does* Sarah Martin miss him her whole life long?"

"Yes, yes, and yes," I said. "Yes, she bears the responsibility. Yes, everyone else forgets him. And yes, she misses him her whole life long."

"You're wrong," Tamar said.

I watched her pick up her miniature artichoke-eating fork and wipe its tiny tines with her napkin.

"You're wrong on all three counts," Tamar said. "One, it wasn't Sarah Martin's responsibility that her brother died. It just happened. Two, Sarah Martin's mother will not ever forget her child. Every minute of every day of her life, she will be remembering the baby she lost."

Tamar pressed the tines of the miniature fork into the back of her hand and studied the marks they left.

"And that's not all," she said. "Sarah Martin's mother will have to watch Sarah Martin be sad. She will not know how to help her child. Worse yet, Sarah Martin's mother will be unable ever to talk about what happened, and that will only make Sarah Martin feel more alone."

Tamar took the empty jar of marinated artichoke hearts to the sink and rinsed it. She came back to the table.

"And you're wrong about something else, too," she said. "Sarah Martin will miss her brother her whole life long, but Sarah Martin will also be happy. She will grow up strong. She will be an amazing adult."

"How?" I said.

"How takes care of itself."

"I'm going to burn these up," I said.

"You'll write more."

"I won't."

"You will," she said. "You can't not."

*Winter Without End* fell back into the box. Tamar got up from the table, went over to the kitchen drawer, and brought back a clean dishcloth. She wiped my face.

I carried the crate out to the burn barrel.

They went quietly to their deaths. They puffed into the air, black words curling into gray ash, spiraling away into the sky. I did not allow myself to think of all that I had imagined, all the families I had put together or torn apart, all the children I had sent on perilous journeys, all the people who never found out what happened.

The old man would have gone north with me, through the Adirondacks, up near the border of Vermont. He would have made the trip with me. I was going to ask him to do that with me, and his reply would have been yes. The old man would have known that I wanted to find a small patch of primeval forest, near the Vermont border. He would have known that all I wanted to do was sit there for one day, sit in the patch of primeval forest. The sun would have shone down on us and slowly made its way across the sky. The old man would have sat with me on the soft moss. He would not have talked unless I asked him an answer-demanding question. He would have sat perfectly still with me, hardly breathing, so that eventually the primeval animals would have thought we were part of the landscape. They would have come forth from the woods, dipping and raising their heads, and gazed upon us with their soft eyes. They would have been curious about these new animals that sat as still as dawn.

Primeval animals have never seen human beings. They don't know yet that humans are to be feared, that they carry guns and traps, that the soft fur of animals is something to be sought and taken.

My hermit grandfather would have scared these animals away. Animals living within a few miles' radius of my hermit grandfather would have known fear, and they would have learned that fear from my hermit grandfather. They would have learned distrust of humans, how to step around their traps, how to melt into the underbrush in the fall and barely breathe as the hermit hunter-trapper glided past, his gun at the ready.

Those primeval animals would have passed that distrust and fear on to their young, and their young would not have been primeval animals. They would have been a new breed of animal, one with human added to their list of enemies.

After the old man died in the fire, my hermit grandfather disappeared. My hermit grandfather, who lived in that patch of primeval forest and traded pelts in the village for bare essentials on his twice-yearly trading trips, no longer lives there. No one knows where he went. He took his tipi, his stored pelts, and his flint with him. His gun and his traps he loaded onto the travois and dragged it away behind him. He found a new life.

After he was gone, the primeval patch of forest grew over the spot where he had lived for those years. Moss crept back over the circle of flattened earth where his tipi had been pitched. Birds eventually grew bold and built their nests in the tops of the towering pines that had shaded his summer camp. Once-primeval animals who still knew the fear of a human being watched and waited until the day came when they knew that my hermit grandfather would not be back, and then one by one they entered his patch of forest. Charred remains of his campfire were covered in one summer by new leaves and grass, and in the winter pine needles lay scattered on the whiteness of the snow in the small clearing. Deer came to nibble on the new growth of the baby apple trees that grew at the edge of the primeval forest, apple trees that had grown from seeds dropped from my hermit grandfather's apple core.

In the village where he had gone twice a year to trade his pelts, the storekeeper thought of him just once, in the spring.

"Where's that old trapper?" he asked his clerk assistant.

"The one with the beaver pelts?"

"Yeah. Isn't this about his time?"

They kept a lookout for my hermit grandfather for a week or so, expecting to see his deerskin jacket appear, his bowed head, the fringe on his pants dirtied by the spring mud. They listened for his voice, unused to words, his yes and his no, his lack of language. What they watched for, what they listened for, did not come.

And no one ever saw my hermit grandfather again.

The old man would have sat quietly with me and felt the sun pass overhead. At the end of the day he would have turned to me and said, "Well?" He would have held out his hand to me, and we would have gotten up together. Our muscles would have been cramped from a day of sitting and not moving, a day of pretending to be primeval animals. We would have walked out of the woods together. The old man would have understood that all I wanted was that one day, one day of seeing the place where my hermit grandfather had lived and breathed and thought his thoughts. One day of mourning. I would never have gone back.

I went back into the house through the garage door. Tamar was in the bathroom, the jar of artichoke hearts emptied and rinsed on the kitchen counter. In my bedroom upstairs I pressed my nose against the cold windowpane and looked out at the freak snow, blue in the darkness, and the light of the moon. Orange light flickered against the blue-white snow and the darkness of the woods. If you were a skier skiing through the foothills of the Adirondacks, on your way north to a patch of primeval forest near Vermont, you would be able to see where you were going by the light of the flames, their fierce heat burning up all the fake book reports I had ever written.

Certain trees need fierce heat to regenerate. Take the lodge-pole pine, for example. Lodgepole pines do not grow in the Adirondacks. Even in a patch of primeval Adirondack forest, you would not find a lodgepole pine. They are high-altitude trees. They're huge. They can grow to be extremely old. But to reproduce, a lodgepole pine needs intense heat. Only then can a lodgepole pine dislodge its seeds. Baby lodgepole pines grow in the charred earth that is left after a forest fire. In order to have a chance at life, baby lodgepole pines must be born in flame. That's not the kind of tree that grows in the Adirondacks.

After I found the rusted pioneer pot, I washed it and dried it to prevent more rust, and I stored it with my metalworking tools. The old man had given me a pair of tin snips and a solder iron. He was going to train me in the art of welding, but we ran out of time. We didn't know that we would run out of time, but we did. I put the rusted metal pioneer pot in the back of my closet, in an old wooden apple crate that Tamar and I found once when we drove up north to Deeper Lake.

My hair is starting to grow in where the burned scalp was. I lift up my fingers sometimes to touch it and feel its featheriness. *It's dead,* I remind myself, but it feels alive and lovely despite its deadness.

In my twelfth year I learned the importance of usefulness as well as beauty. I began to see consistency among that which is inconsistent. I came to understand the art of possibility. Those were the ways that the old man had saved his life, and they are what he taught me. I was his apprentice, and he was the master.

The first night I ever saw the old man, black shapes moved through the trees, like shadows or bats flying low. I didn't see the old man at first. He moved behind light. Orange flame flickered in front of him. Something black behind the flame was what I stared at. The black shape bent and leaned, curved and straightened. I knew I was watching a metalworker. I knew that he was lighting lanterns.

The old man would be dead before the next winter was out. I didn't know that then. That's part of what being an apprentice means. An apprentice might be set loose at any time. She has to go on alone, remembering what the master taught her. She has to be able to see the world as separate but connected parts, joined not by letters and words but by relationships, and the possibility of beauty.

That first night all I knew was that someone in Nine Mile Woods was joining metal together, lighting up the forest. He was making something useful, something beautiful and full of possibility for the people passing by in the woods, something that I couldn't yet see or understand. But I was a child then.

# Reading Group Guide

1. One of the underlying themes in *Shadow Baby* is art—what it is, the people who make it, the people who appreciate it. (Think about, for example, Clara's soliloquy on book reports versus actual books.) Clara believes that the old man has taught her the "art of possibility, and the possibility of beauty." What do you think the book is saying about the process of creating art? What are your own feelings on that subject?

2. In many ways the novel is a study in opposites. For example, Clara lives for words, while the old man is illiterate. In what ways do such contrasts serve to illuminate and deepen Clara's understanding of life?

3. In what ways do Clara's fake book reports mirror her world? In what ways do they represent her inner psyche? Why does she burn them all up in the end?

4. *Shadow Baby* opens with this line, "Now that the old man is gone, I think about him much of the time." Clara is twelve

years old as she narrates the book, looking back on the past year of her life. Because she is still very young, she is not capable of having a long perspective of time, yet the book ends with this line: "But I was a child then." Think about other fictional child narrators, for example, Holden Caulfield in *The Catcher in the Rye* and Laura Ingalls in the Little House books, and discuss the events behind their transition into adulthood. Compare and contrast them to Clara.

5. Clara's mother, Tamar, practices weekly in a church choir. Yet Tamar never attends church, nor do the old man or Clara. Is there nonetheless some religious significance in the book?

6. What is the significance of the title?

7. While it is true that the mother-daughter relationship in the novel is difficult, did you find it believable and real? Why does Tamar refuse to answer Clara's questions?

8. To Clara, "real life" is often indistinguishable from her fantasy life. What purpose does her wild imagination serve?

9. The story of Clara's relationship with CJ Wilson is intertwined with the story of her chickens. How do the two stories both reflect and enlarge each other?

10. In the book, one person looks at a dented tin can and sees garbage, another looks at the same can and sees the possibility of beauty in the form of a lantern or cookie cutters. How does the book play with ideas of how individual ways of seeing influence one's experience of the world?

11. Clara is obsessed with pioneers and their stories of incredible hardship and triumph over adversity. Can the book be viewed as a metaphor (or possibly an anti-metaphor) for the traditional American mythology surrounding its immigrant past?

12. Think about the opening scene of the book in which Clara glimpses the old man hanging lanterns in the woods. Think about the ending scene in which she is burning her fake book reports in the snow. How do these two scenes, which "bookend" the novel, mirror each other? What do they tell us about how Clara has changed in the interim?